Denne was almost numb with panic now that 3:30 had really arrived—her first tutoring session with Michael!

Michael is my student and Alicia's boyfriend, she thought. *I'll just have to forget him*. But she knew that a decision made with her head wou... able to control her hear... and shaking as she l... Michael wasn't com...

Just then the door op... moment just inside th... looked into his eyes fo... Denne couldn't breat... movement would brea... spell.

Nothing existed except Michael. . . .

Dear Reader,

At Silhouette we publish books with you in mind. We're pleased to announce the creation of Silhouette First Love, a new line of contemporary romances written by the finest young-adult writers as well as outstanding new authors in this field.

Silhouette First Love captures many of the same elements enjoyed by Silhouette Romance readers—love stories, happy endings and the same attention to detail and description. But First Love features young heroines and heroes in contemporary and recognizable situations.

You play an important part in our future plans for First Love. We welcome any suggestions or comments on our books and I invite you to write to us at the address below.

Jane Nicholls
Silhouette Books
PO Box 177
Dunton Green
Sevenoaks
Kent
TN13 2YE

IN MY SISTER'S SHADOW

Genell Dellin

First Love from Silhouette
Published by Silhouette Books

First printing 1983

British Library C.I.P.

Dellin, Genell
In my sister's shadow.—(Silhouette first love)
I. Title
813'.54[F] PS3554.E/

ISBN 0 340 33682 X

The characters and situations in this book are entirely imaginary and bear no relation to any real person or actual happening

Printed and bound in Great Britain for Hodder and Stoughton Paperbacks, a division of Hodder and Stoughton Ltd., Mill Road, Dunton Green, Sevenoaks, Kent (Editorial Office: 47 Bedford Square, London, WC1 3DP) by Richard Clay (The Chaucer Press) Ltd., Bungay, Suffolk

For Ara Robinson Gill,
my grandmother and teacher
And in loving memory of Grady Gill,
my grandfather and friend

1

Denne saw him the minute she walked into the main hallway where the tables were set up for enrollment. He had his back to her, but she would have recognized him anywhere, even in a crowd much larger than this. The confident way he held his broad shoulders, the smooth sheen of his blond hair, and the way his head was tilted as he listened to the girl beside him were all unmistakable.

Denne stopped just inside the door, afraid that if he saw her and spoke to her she'd blush deep red and completely lose her voice. That's what she usually did if their paths crossed when he came to pick up her sister, Alicia. She stood transfixed, her whole body almost trembling as if she were scared or cold. She felt warm, though, at the same time, and too weak to move on toward the table marked "Juniors, A–D."

For the thousandth time Denne thought what a

lucky girl Alicia was. Not only was she pretty and popular and a leader in practically every activity in school, but she was also dating Michael Long, perfect person.

"Hi, Denne! You're late; I thought you'd never get here . . . Denne?" Sharon broke Denne's reverie, bubbling with her usual enthusiasm, her frizzy red hair bouncing on her shoulders.

"What are you standing over here for? We need to get in line or all the classes will be full and we won't even get lunch hour together!" Sharon tugged at Denne's arm in her haste to get the school year arranged to her satisfaction.

"Oh, Sharon, hi!" Denne finally noticed her friend.

"I've been standing over there waving to you for ages," Sharon went on, "but you were in a world of your own. What were you looking at, anyway?"

Denne's stomach tightened with fear that Sharon might guess her secret. Sharon was her best friend, true, and she shared almost everything with her, but not this. The feelings of excitement that Michael stirred in her were too strong and confusing and somehow much too personal to mention to anyone. Besides, he was her sister's boyfriend, just an unreachable ideal, like Billy Joel or Rod Stewart.

She turned to Sharon with a smile, forcing her voice to be casual. "Oh, nothing. I guess it just hit me that junior year is actually about to begin."

"It certainly is, and I can't wait," Sharon declared, with her usual zest for living. "I just have a feeling it's going to be the best year yet. I'll bet we're even going to get boyfriends this year!"

Denne replied with a wry smile, "I'm sure,

Sharon. I just know we'll break all the hearts on the football team!"

As they moved to get into line, Denne sneaked one more glance in Michael's direction, but he was gone.

When it finally was their turn, Mrs. Ulrich really tried to enroll Sharon and Denne in at least one class together, but finally she gave up.

"It's impossible, girls. You have to have band, Sharon, and you want the art class in oils, Denne, plus French Literature, so that forces you into different English and social studies classes. There's just no way."

Sharon sighed dramatically. "Little did I know when I said it, but we *are* lucky to have lunch hour together!"

"I know," Denne moaned, "and I'm glad for that, but I just hate the thought of going into all those new classes by myself! I have a feeling that this year I'm going to need all the help I can get!"

Clutching their schedule cards, the two girls walked slowly down the wide hallway, glancing into the classrooms on each side. In spite of her worries, Denne began to feel the upsurge of excitement she always felt at the beginning of a new school year.

"I love the beginning of school!" Denne exclaimed, stopping in the doorway of Mme Clouet's room, her wide brown eyes slowly taking it all in.

"Just look how neat the room is—the desks are all in perfect rows, the floor is shining, the bulletin boards are all fresh, even the chalk is new!"

"I know, and so is my band instrument; Mr. Branson ordered all new clarinets. Listen, I think I'll run down there and check it out and talk to him for a minute. Wait for me at the front door and we'll walk home together, O.K.?"

"O.K."

Sharon rushed off in the direction of the band room and Denne wandered into the familiar world of French class. The room was still and peaceful and Denne felt her confidence returning. At least I'll have one class I won't mind coming into by myself, she thought. French class will be like arts camp all over again, except even better. I'll bet I'm the only student from Clinton who spent the summer speaking French, so at least in this one class I'll be special! Regretfully, Denne sighed. If only she could be special in everything, in school and out, just like Alicia.

One wall of the classroom was covered with a long bulletin board; Mme Clouet had hung the French flag at one end, the American Flag at the other. In between she'd stapled travel posters and brightly colored maps. All the red, white and blue reflecting in the sunlight shining on the desk tops filled Denne with a sudden surge of patriotism for both countries, and she moved to look closely at the posters thinking, What a thrill it would be to go to France, to actually see and feel and experience it!

The biggest poster was a stunning picture of a castlelike building on a promontory jutting up out of a seemingly boundless sea. The permanence and mystery that the ancient building held drew Denne's thoughts again, even though she had looked at pictures of it many times. She tried to let the picture absorb her, attempting to imagine herself walking through the halls of the venerable abbey. Sometimes she could almost feel as if she were there, but today her eyes kept straying to the name printed in large blue letters across the bottom of the poster: Mont-St.-Michel.

The word Michel rang in her mind, but instead of an age-old French monastery, her mind was filled with a seventeen-year-old boy, tall and blond, with large brown eyes and a slow and thoughtful smile.

"Michel," she whispered to herself, trying the sound in her ears and the feel of the word on her tongue. How she would love to say it to him and have him look at her the way he sometimes looked at Alicia. An almost physical pain shot through her with the thought, and Denne forced herself to think about something else.

I need to look for something new to do this year, she reflected. A hobby. Maybe the oil painting class will be really fun and make me want to paint all the time. Or maybe I'll find a whole new activity. And for sure, I'm still going to get good grades, better than ever, especially in *le français!*

That was the one area in their lives in which she could outshine Alicia. The idea consoled her for a moment, then she thought bitterly, Big deal! Who have I ever impressed by making A's except my parents and a few teachers? Being on the honor roll is about as important on the scale of social values at Clinton High as being double-jointed.

Restlessly Denne walked out of the classroom and started toward the front door of the building, wondering whether Sharon had finished talking with Mr. Branson. By the time she reached the main lobby area Sharon's red head was nowhere in sight, and most of the students who had been milling around there earlier had gone. Denne waved to Mrs. Ulrich who was just gathering her things to leave the enrollment table and, in order to have something to do while she waited, walked over to read the bulletin board notices that were posted just outside the main office door.

A neatly hand-lettered sign caught her eye:

ARE YOU GOOD AT SOMETHING OTHER PEOPLE AREN'T?

WANT TO HELP?

WE NEED TUTORS IN:

MATH	LATIN
CHEMISTRY	FRENCH
GRAMMAR	BIOLOGY

IF YOU ARE GOOD AT ONE OR MORE OF THE ABOVE SUBJECTS AND WOULD LIKE TO HELP ANOTHER STUDENT, SEE MRS. KIRBY BEFORE FRIDAY, SEPTEMBER 11.

Denne read the notice twice.

This could be just the thing! she thought. It would be a new activity and it would give me even more practice in French than I'll get just in class. I'll need that if I'm going to keep the fluency I worked so hard for at camp this summer. She tried to imagine her student. Who would sign up for help in French? Probably some really slow freshman girl who could hardly speak English any better than she could French. She'll probably be so dumb she'll drive me crazy, Denne thought, but so what? After all, if I can't be popular, I might as well be useful!

Quickly Denne went through the door to the main office and walked up to the counter. Mrs. Kirby, the principal's secretary, looked up from her typewriter in her usual impatient way.

"Yes, may I help you?"

"I want to sign up for tutoring, please, in French. I . . . I mean, I want to *be* a tutor, not sign up for tutoring," she stammered. Good grief, get hold of yourself, she thought. You're not applying to teach a whole class, just one simple little freshman who is, no doubt, scared out of her mind just to be in high school.

Mrs. Kirby came to the counter with a card, and stood watching while Denne filled in the blanks.

As soon as she printed "Denne Drake" in the first space, Mrs. Kirby exclaimed, "Drake! Do you know Alicia Drake? She's one of our most outstanding seniors."

Denne stopped writing, her concentration broken. "I know," she said, "she's my sister."

"Your sister?" Mrs. Kirby's voice held the disbelieving tones Denne had come to expect with those words. "Well, you girls certainly don't look much alike, do you?"

Denne didn't look up. "I suppose not," she muttered, continuing to fill in the blanks.

When she had finished, Mrs. Kirby took the card and tapped its edge on the shiny work surface while she gave Denne an appraising stare.

"We'll check your grades and ask the teachers you've listed here for references," she informed her briskly, "and if you are approved, we'll assign your student to you tomorrow. You came in just in time; we want to get all the assignments made and tutoring sessions started next week during the first week of classes." She turned to go back to her desk.

"Oh, Mrs. Kirby," Denne called, "how do I know who my student is and when and where we're supposed to meet?"

"Just come by here anytime during the day on

Monday and I'll have that information typed out for you."

"All right. Thank you."

Denne went back into the hallway to find Sharon waiting at the front door.

"What've you been doing in there?" she teased. "Did you get sent to the office before school has even started?"

Denne smiled and pulled her friend out into the warm afternoon.

"Sharon, you'll never believe it, but I have a whole new career!" Denne turned and walked backward in front of Sharon so she could watch her reaction to the news.

"I am now a teacher. I've just signed up to tutor someone who's having trouble with French," she announced.

Sharon's blue eyes opened wide.

"You are? You have? Who? Who will be your student? That's great Denne, I'll bet you'll really like that! I think it'd be fun. Just think, you'll be the one who makes the assignments and gives the tests and everything! What a welcome change! But won't it take a lot of time? When are you going to do it?"

Denne laughed. "Sharon, that reaction is so typical of you—old get 'em organized Sharon! I don't know any of the details, I'll find all that out on Monday."

"Well, just don't let it interfere with our lunch hours or we'll practically never see each other again."

"Oh, I'm sure we wouldn't meet during lunch, Sharon, don't worry. I'm not worried about that; I just want to know who will be my student. It'll probably be some silly little freshman who doesn't have a brain in her head!"

Sharon was still more interested in schedules. "It can't interfere with lunch and it can't take too much of your spare time in general, because you will have to have time for all our double dates. I'm perfectly serious, Denne, I have decided that this year we are both going to start dating. In fact, I think we'll just go steady with two guys who also happen to be best friends. That would be neat, don't you think?"

Denne chuckled. "Sharon, will you face reality? Maybe you are going to get a boyfriend, but I'm not. I can't figure out how to relate to the simplest boy. I'm friends with Jeff Watson because we have sat next to each other in French for the past four years, but I hardly ever even talk to any other boys, and I blush whenever I get into any situation that is a boy-girl kind of thing. I'll never get used to it," she mused ruefully.

The girls had stopped at the corner of Evans Road and Maple because Sharon was going to turn toward her house. She shook her fuzzy head at Denne and grinned defiantly.

"We'll see, Denne, we'll see. You know how I can be when I'm determined, and I have absolutely made up my mind about this!" She turned and marched down Maple Street, leaving Denne standing at the corner.

2

Denne took her time walking along Evans Road under the arching elm trees. The sun felt warm on her shoulders when it could reach her between the leaves. It's just like summer, still, she thought. I think I'll pretend summer is never going to end; this has been the best summer of my whole life and I don't want to ruin it with a school year full of problems. She began to hum the theme from *Can-Can,* the play the French Colony had given the last night of arts camp, the play in which Denne had been the star.

I'll never, never forget that, she promised herself. That was the greatest feeling; attention, applause, performing in front of so many people and knowing that I was doing it well. She smiled to herself as images from the summer floated through her head: M and Mme Drousseau telling everyone that she had a natural talent for the language and a greater facility for it than any other camper there; Ron Hartman playing opposite her and talking to her at the cast party where she was still in her beautiful costume; other campers asking her to help them with their accents. Oh, it had been great!

It had been great for another reason, too. There had been no Alicia at camp, nobody there had made comparisons; they had seen Denne as just herself. That was probably one reason I felt so free, Denne thought. For the first time in my life I wasn't trying to live up to somebody's expectations of what Alicia's sister should be like, and I loved every minute of it!

Still humming, Denne went up the broad front steps and let herself into the house. It was quiet, and as she closed the door she called, "Mom? Alicia? Anybody home?"

She received two answers: a faint call from upstairs and the scratching noise of Muffin's toenails on the polished wood floor of the hall as the playful cocker spaniel rushed to greet Denne. She stooped to scratch her behind the ears just as Alicia appeared, rushing down the stairs on her way out of the house.

"Oh, hi, Denne," she said breathlessly. "Did you get enrolled O.K.?"

"Yes, I think I got all the classes I needed, but Sharon and I . . ."

"Look, I wish I could hear all about it," Alicia interrupted, "but Julie's waiting—the guys are picking us up after football practice and we're going to celebrate our last free weekend before school starts." She put her hand on the doorknob and turned to give Denne her most dazzling smile. "Tell Mom I'll probably be in late, will you?" she asked.

Denne nodded, thinking that anyone who looked like that could get away with staying out late or anything else she wanted. Alicia was dressed in crisp yellow slacks and a paler yellow top made of a gauzy fabric. It matched her hair almost exactly and set off her dark blue eyes to perfection. With a wave, she was gone.

Denne turned back to Muffin. "Well, old girl, I can see why people say I don't look much like my sister, can't you?" she asked.

Muffin followed as Denne went upstairs and changed from her new jeans and short-sleeved blue velour top into her oldest and most comfortable cut-offs and T-shirt. She pulled the soft red cotton shirt over her head and went to the old dresser she'd refinished last year to pick up her hairbrush. As she ran the brush through the masses of short dark curls that fit her head like a shiny cap, Denne looked into the mirror. Looking back at her was a slim, tanned face with a straight nose and wide dark eyes. She stared appraisingly at her reflection for several seconds.

"Hmm, doesn't look much like a star to me now," she muttered softly, putting the brush down and turning toward the door.

The dog stayed right at her heels back down the stairs again and into the kitchen, and sat begging while Denne went through the big bowl of fruit on the butcher block trying to find just the right apple. She always chose the red delicious ones that still had lots of green on them. They tasted much better because they weren't mellow yet, and besides that, they were interesting to look at. Denne loved the shadings of red into yellow and green and, sometimes right at the stem, almost blue, and the way the colors flowed around the shape of the fruit.

At last she found one that was perfect. She tossed it up and turned to Muffin, pretending that she'd just noticed her pleading eyes and paws. She reached into the cabinet.

"Oh, O.K., here's your Milk-bone, Muffin, now let's go outside."

That was a great idea, according to Muffin's wagging tail, and she was the first one out the door. Denne headed straight for the big maple tree; it had been her special spot in the whole backyard for as long as she could remember. When she was little she had climbed in it and played with her toys beneath it, and once, when she was in about the sixth grade, she and Alicia had even started a tree house in it. Alicia had lost interest quickly, though, and Denne couldn't do it all alone, so the tree house had never come to be, and Denne's father had installed a hammock instead.

Denne settled herself into the hammock, propping her head up with the denim-covered pillow so she could eat her apple. Muffin curled up into a ball on the ground and began to chew on the dog biscuit.

Denne tried to continue her memories of the summer, but they refused to come back. She gave up, and pushing herself very gently with one toe, making the hammock move at exactly the right slow pace back and forth, back and forth, she let her mind float into the colors and shapes above her.

Summer must have at least a thousand different shades of green, she thought, and this tree has a sample of every one of them. Her eyes drifted among the leaves, picking out specific colors from the paint set on her desk upstairs: that one is leaf green mixed with cadmium yellow with a touch of Prussian blue. That one is more brilliant yellow light and a little cadmium red pale. That one looks like an apple—medium green shading into dark red.

Reds, yellows, more reds, she noticed, as her brown eyes moved rapidly from leaf to leaf. Soon they'll all be turned, and the greens will be gone. The greens will be gone and so will the summer. No, not will be. The summer is gone. I might as well face it. After all, I enrolled this morning.

My junior year is here, she thought, I have to face the fact that I'm going to be compared with Alicia more than ever because the seniors are involved in almost every activity that the juniors have. And no matter what Sharon says about getting boyfriends through determination, there's no way I can get one that can compare with Alicia's.

That thought brought back the vision of Michael in the hallway at school that morning, and the hurt and excitement and panic that he always aroused in Denne all came flooding back. Suddenly, she saw an image of him the first time she'd ever seen him, standing on the front steps with Alicia last winter, dressed in his black tuxedo, looking down at Alicia, beautiful in a long white dress. Their clothes were a contrast, but their shining blond heads were a perfect match in front of the big wreath of holly and pinecones that Denne's mother had used to trim the door.

Denne had stood watching with her mother while her father took pictures, and her mother had squeezed her hand and whispered, "Next year that'll be you!" Denne had known right then that it wouldn't be the same if she wasn't with Michael.

She had also known that it probably wouldn't even be her; how was she suddenly going to get a date for the Winter Dinner Dance when she'd never had a real date in her life?

Looking up into the gently stirring leaves, Denne felt the tension inside her twisting and turning the way the wind moved the leaves. "That time's actually coming, Muffin, coming in just a few short months, and I don't know what I'll do," she murmured, the apple forgotten in her hand. "I don't know how in the world I'll get a date; no matter what Sharon says. Face it, there are some things that determination can't fix."

No, determination won't do it, she thought. What I need is what Alicia has, *that* will do it every time. She is so totally beautiful, with her gleaming golden hair and big blue eyes and that figure with all the curves in the right places. She always knows exactly what to say and how to look at a boy and how to make him laugh. I don't have any of that, and I don't know any of that. I have talked to Jeff Watson for four years, and I don't have the foggiest idea of how to get him to ask me out.

"Not that I want Jeff Watson to take me to the Dinner Dance," she informed Muffin, who was listening carefully. "It's not that, Muffin. I know now just as I knew the minute I saw him that no boy but Michael could make that magic feeling for me. I want to go to the Winter Dinner Dance with Michael!"

But Alicia will go with him to that dance just as surely as she will be homecoming queen, Denne thought painfully. She'll be with Michael at the dance, she'll be homecoming queen, she'll star in the junior-senior play, she'll be everywhere I turn this whole year long, and I will hate it. I cannot stand very many more times for someone to say to me, "I can't believe *you're* Alicia Drake's *sister!*" or "You girls certainly don't look alike, do you?" Oh, why couldn't she be one more year older so she'd be gone before I was a junior?

Muffin was sympathetic, but she had no answers.

Fiercely, Denne bit into the apple and finished it off. The colors in the leaves were beginning to fade just a little as the sun started to drop behind the big tree. Its enormous shadow fell across the grass, and as Denne sat up and looked toward the house she saw how it seemed to engulf the whole yard. Muffin romped out into it, and Denne laughed unhappily.

"You look the way I feel in my sister's shadow, Muff, slightly overwhelmed."

She got up and went into the house.

Denne spent the long weekend thinking that perhaps Monday wouldn't come, but it did. She woke very early and lay in bed for a little while, watching the light get stronger through the thin gauze curtains that were gathered over her windows. She lay there so long, daydreaming, that when she finally did get up, Alicia was in the bathroom they shared. Denne flipped through all her clothes again while she waited, although she had carefully chosen her first-day-of-school outfit the night before. After considering and discarding several things, she decided to stick with her original choice; chocolate brown corduroy jeans, brown, gold and white plaid shirt, and gold sweater to tie around her shoulders; though the day would probably be too hot for a sweater later on.

Denne finally got the bathroom and dressed and went downstairs to pretend to eat breakfast.

"Hi, Mom. Where's everybody else?"

"Dad had to go in early and Michael picked Alicia up half an hour ago. What would you like, eggs? pancakes?" Denne's mother smiled at her brightly.

Denne smiled back, a little shakily. "Mom, you know me. First day of school jitters. Juice and toast will be fine."

She drank the juice, and played with the toast for a few minutes while pretending to listen to her mother outlining her plans for the day. Finally Denne stood up.

"Gotta go, Mom. Don't want to be late the first day."

Denne *was* almost late, though, and she realized it as soon as she turned the corner and saw that there were no students standing around outside the main door and very few of them going into the building. She quickened her pace and ran up the steps just as the big clock overhead in the hallway showed 7:55.

Oh, I have five minutes, she thought, looking at the main office door. I could find out who my student is; Mrs. Kirby said come by any time on Monday.

Denne pushed open the office door and moved past some students who were just enrolling in order to get up to the counter. She stood uneasily, wondering if she would be able to get Mrs. Kirby's attention soon, so she could be on time for class.

Just then the secretary saw her and started going through a stack of cards on her desk. Mrs. Kirby might be brusque and impatient, but she was efficient to a fault. She rose and came to the counter.

"Here's your card, Denne. If you have any questions come back and see me," she said, as she turned to help one of the new students with a form he was filling out.

Denne took the card, glanced at it, and stood rooted to the floor. She felt dizzy and weak and completely helpless. Somewhere in the back of her mind she thought, I'll never make it to class today, much less on time. I'll never be able to move again.

The words on the small white card in her hand leaped out at her: STUDENT: MICHAEL LONG.

3

Denne never knew how she made it to homeroom; she didn't even remember leaving the office. Somehow, though, she found herself sitting in Mrs. Henderson's classroom with the fateful card still clutched in her hand. Mrs. Henderson was reading the announcements for the day, but none of the words got past the roaring in Denne's ears. She looked at the small black words on the stiff white paper again, and this time she read them all:

> STUDENT: MICHAEL LONG
> SCHEDULE: MONDAYS AND THURSDAYS, ROOM 113
> FIRST MEETING: MONDAY, SEPTEMBER 14, 3:30 P.M.

That was today! This afternoon after school she was to meet Michael alone! How would she ever get through the day? It was harrowing enough to go to all new classes without Sharon and now on top of that she had to have enough composure to talk to Michael without making a fool of herself!

Suddenly all the other students got up and began moving toward the door, so Denne left her seat and joined them. She forced her brain to start functioning again, at least enough to tell her which class she had next.

She went into Mrs. Ulrich's English class, took a seat, and opened her notebook to write down assignments without a single thought for who was sitting near her or whether anyone had noticed her or spoken to her. Well, she thought wryly, at least I'm not worried anymore about being shy in class. Now I can just worry about being shy after school!

Denne completely forgot about Michael and being shy, though, as soon as Mrs. Ulrich started to lecture.

"We'll open this semester with our study of Shakespeare. I want to do this early in the semester because our junior-senior play this year will be a production of *As You Like It* and I think all of you will enjoy it much more if you are familiar with Shakespeare and the time period in which he wrote. Those of you who are *in* the play, of course, should give even better performances because of that background. . . ."

Wouldn't it be fun to be in the play? Denne thought. She loved Shakespeare and she had loved acting in the French play this summer; maybe she should try out. But it's the junior-senior play, she reminded herself, and Alicia will no doubt be the star. I certainly can't compete with her—if I tried out I'd probably get the part of her maid!

Denne concentrated on the rest of the lecture, took some notes, and checked out her new textbook all the while keeping her thoughts on the business at hand. As soon as class was over, though, and she was out in the crowded hallway again, the panic came back. She made her way in the general direction of art class with Michael's name reverberating through her head, and when she happened to run into Sharon, her first impulse was to blurt out the news. She opened her mouth, but she didn't get a chance to say a thing.

"Denne, hi! Guess what! I have the most exciting thing to tell you!"

A tall boy pushed away a crowd of students around his locker, and Sharon was carried with them down the hall from Denne. She managed to call back, "Now you'll have to believe what I tell you. I'll give you the proof at lunchtime!"

What is that girl talking about? Denne thought. Well, if she weren't all excited about something, she wouldn't be Sharon. Shrugging, Denne went into art class and found a seat by the window.

That entire class was a blur. She must have at least appeared to be listening, since Mr. Sloane didn't say anything to her, but she had no idea what he was talking about. All she could think about was 3:30 P.M. and what she would say to Michael. How can I help him with French when I can't even talk to him in English? she agonized. Everytime he came to the house for Alicia when they first started dating he had always spoken to Denne and tried to strike up a conversation. She was invariably tongue-tied, however, and now she simply avoided being around when he came. That didn't keep her from watching him, though. She always managed to get a glimpse of his wide shoulders as he walked in his confident way up to the door or she watched him escort Alicia to the car and swing into the seat behind the wheel with that quick, assured gesture. It depressed her, then, when Alicia scooted over very close to Michael as they drove away.

Well, I'm always wanting to be the one sitting with him and this afternoon I'll get my wish, she thought. There I'll be, sitting with him—staring, struck dumb.

Mr. Sloane stopped talking just as the bell rang and Denne got up and hurried toward government class. As she moved through the students in the corridor she speculated about whether Mr. Walker really would give homework the first day as he was rumored to do. Mr. Walker had a reputation for being the strictest teacher at Clinton and everyone was a little afraid of him; Denne certainly didn't want to be late to his class the first day. Michael moved to the back of her mind, and after class began she forgot him entirely.

That was because Mr. Walker started right in, just as people had done ever since Denne could remember. He was calling the roll, and as soon as he said "Denne Drake" he stopped the roll call and said, "Denne, are you related to Alicia Drake? She was one of my students last year."

"Yes, she's my sister."

"Your sister? Well, great. Alicia was very active in student council and all of its activities and I'm sure you will be, too. It's wonderful to have people who want to work for the school."

Mr. Walker continued roll call.

Well, there's one good thing, at least, Denne thought. He didn't get that shocked tone in his voice when I said Alicia was my sister, in fact, he's the one who suggested we might be related!

Denne's relief was short-lived, though, because as soon as Mr. Walker finished roll call and checked out the textbooks, he returned to the subject of student council and the upcoming election of representatives.

"Let's have someone run from this class, and we'll all help in the campaign. It will be a practical lesson in politics, and we'll get a good person elected that way!"

Mr. Walker was warming to his subject, getting very enthusiastic. "All right, now, who will volunteer to run for junior representative?"

He looked around for hands in the air. "Remember, this is a good opportunity to serve your school."

No one responded. Mr. Walker's eyes moved carefully all around the room again, then they came back toward the front. Denne felt them on her, and she had a sinking feeling.

Her fears were confirmed. In his most persuasive voice Mr. Walker said, "Denne, why don't you run for the council? Alicia was a very energetic representative for us last year, and I'm sure you will be, too."

Denne wanted to fade into the floor.

"I . . . Mr. Walker, I don't think . . ."

Mr. Walker went right on. "Of course you will. That's great. I knew you'd want to do something for the school. Thank you, Denne. Now, we just need to begin organizing the campaign; we have very little time before the election. The first thing we'll need is a campaign manager."

A girl sitting across the aisle from Denne raised her hand.

"I'll be manager, Mr. Walker. I'd like to do that "

"All right, Jan, fine. Thank you very much."

Denne was astounded. How had all this happened? She had no desire to run for student council or anything else; she couldn't imagine going around asking for votes and making speeches.

"The first thing you need to do is write your speech for assembly, Denne. Jan, you can help, and when you get it ready you can practice it in this class. Remember, now, the campaign assembly is in a few days, so you don't have long to get prepared."

Speech for assembly! How could I possibly get up in front of the entire student body and make a speech? Denne worried. I'll just have to tell him that I don't want to do this, that I *can't* do it.

Tentatively, Denne raised her hand and tried to get Mr. Walker's attention, but he was going on to a new subject, the syllabus for the semester, and he ignored her. He began dictating dates and the subjects to be covered, and Denne had to concentrate on taking notes. It was murder if a student asked Mr. Walker for information he had already given.

After class Denne tried again, but students were swarming around the desk, and she had to hurry if she were to meet Sharon on time for lunch. With a sinking feeling, she gave up and left the room, trying to resign herself to the fact that she was now running for junior representative.

Sharon was waiting in the cafeteria. The two girls

moved quickly into line, both bursting with news, but it was noisy and too rushed for talking. As soon as they had their food and were settled at a table, Sharon blurted,

"Denne, it's happened! Just because I was determined, it has now happened!"

"*What* has happened, Sharon? Will you please tell me what you're talking about?" Denne was exasperated. She had so much to tell, too, and they only had a few minutes to talk.

Sharon took a bite of hamburger to delay her dramatic moment, put the sandwich down, and deliberately touched her napkin to her mouth. Denne shook her arm.

"Tell me this minute or you won't get a chance; I have something to tell you, too!"

Sharon gave in. "I've met him. I have already met the boy I'm going to date this year and it's only the first day of school. I can hardly believe it myself."

Denne was astonished. "Well, go on. Tell me. Oh, by the way, how do you know you're going to date him? Has he asked you out yet?"

"As a matter of fact, yes, but we'll come to that. I want to tell you exactly how it happened."

Denne stared at her friend, totally amazed, through a ten-minute description of the events leading up to the magic moment in band class. She tried to pick out the important points because Sharon was indeed telling her, with the minutest of details, *exactly* what had happened.

". . . so when I turned around to talk to Becky, my horn hit the music stand and spilled all the scores on the floor. He kept the stand from falling and . . ."

Denne's imagination leaped from the music stand to student council to Michael. "Come on, Sharon, hurry! I have to talk to you."

"O.K., O.K. I'll tell you the rest on the phone tonight. Anyway, his name is Joe Conley and he has medium brown hair and hazel eyes and a medium build (he's taller than I am, though). Really, he's just medium in every way, except that I think he's really cute. He wants to go for a Coke today after school, so I said yes. Now, Denne, can you *believe* this? I told you I'd made up my mind. All I did was decide I was going to get a boyfriend, and I did! I know he'll ask me out again and that he'll be my boyfriend this year, see?" Sharon's hair seemed to grow more intensely red as the fervor in her voice increased. She grasped Denne's arm and gazed into her eyes. "See? Now all we have to do is find yours—I decided for both of us, remember? You're going to get a boyfriend this year, too. Have you seen anybody today who . . . "

Denne's giggle came rolling out and changed into a laugh as she compared all the tensions and worries of her morning with Sharon's big adventure. "No, Sharon, all morning I didn't see one boy I want to date."

As she stopped laughing and looked affectionately at her friend, she had a sudden impulse to tell Sharon that she really didn't think she even wanted a boyfriend if she couldn't have Michael. She wanted to tell Sharon she'd be seeing and talking with Michael that very afternoon and that would be enough excitement for her. So much excitement, in fact, that she wouldn't know how to cope with it. Somehow, though, she couldn't even mention his name. It just stirred up too many feelings inside her that she didn't even understand, so how could she talk about them with Sharon?

Sharon was looking at Denne as if she'd like to read her mind. "I really don't see how you can laugh, Denne. You didn't believe me Friday, and you might have laughed then, but now you can't. I have proof that my theory works, and you have to admit that I'm right. So, you might as well pick him out, because you are getting a boyfriend!" She leaned back in her chair and folded her arms as if that settled the entire matter. "Now, what was it you were in such a fit to tell me? If it's not a boy, what is it?"

"Sharon, Mr. Walker is making me run for student council, and I'm going to have to have a campaign and a speech in assembly and everything! I will simply die! There is no way that I can give a speech in front of the entire student body. I just can't!"

"Denne, Mr. Walker can't *make* you run for student council, and yes, you *can* make a speech if you just put your mind to it." Denne was afraid she was about to get another lecture on positive thinking, but Sharon looked thoughtful. "I heard Patty Evans is running for junior representative, too."

Denne clapped her hand to her forehead. "Patty Evans! Is that my opponent? Oh, Sharon, there's no way I can beat Patty Evans—she's a cheerleader and everything!"

"Well, you'll notice that I didn't say you could win—I said you could make a speech. I hate to admit it, but there's a limit to what even the strongest determination can do," Sharon replied mournfully.

The warning bell rang, and the girls returned their trays and went to their lockers for the afternoon's supply of books and notebooks.

"Have fun on your date with Joe," Denne called as they parted.

"I will," Sharon beamed. "I'm sorry we won't get to walk home together, though."

"That's O.K., I couldn't anyway. I have to tutor Michael Long after school," Denne threw over her shoulder as she moved away. She glanced back to see Sharon's reaction, and the look of surprise on her face was so complete that it made Denne smile all the way to chemistry class.

4

Chemistry and computer math went by somehow. Denne took notes, wrote down assignments, and alternated worrying about Michael and Patty Evans. Most of the time, however, she had to think about class. This year was going to be hard; five solids were bad enough, and the five Denne had chosen all had a lot of homework involved. I don't know why I was looking for extra activities like tutoring, Denne muttered to herself on the way to French class. I think just my schoolwork is going to take every minute of my time.

Denne went into French class, feeling a lift in her spirits as soon as she entered the room. Mme Clouet was stacking stiff new textbooks on her desk; she had recruited Jeff Watson to help pass them out.

"Ah, *Denise, ma chère! Ça va?*" Mme Clouet was so glad to see Denne that she came around the desk to give her a little hug. Her dark eyes sparkled as she told Denne to choose a seat and then come to help her and Jeff. Everyone was speaking only French, and that made Denne feel good, too. It almost seemed like camp again.

All the memories really started coming back as soon as everyone had a book and class was beginning. Mme Clouet began by asking all the students to tell about their summers in French so that they could start getting the rust off the language. Denne was thrilled that she could tell all about her experiences in fluent French, only getting stuck for vocabulary words twice. Mme Clouet was very excited that Denne's camp experience had been so rewarding. She kept saying, *"Très bien, Denise, très bien!"* in her lilting voice, beaming with satisfaction at the performance of her star pupil.

Denne felt her confidence flowing back as she listened to the other students and realized that, indeed, she would be the best French student this year. It felt good to be sure of herself in *something,* today; every time she thought about Patty Evans or about the meeting with Michael that was looming closer every second, she just wanted to go home and hide.

Too soon, the 3:25 bell rang, and Mme Clouet dismissed the class. She stopped Denne on her way out of the room.

"Denise, tu aideras Michel avec le français?" she asked.

Denne started. How did Mme Clouet know that she would be tutoring Michael? she wondered. Then she realized that the French teacher was probably the one who had matched them up; if not, she at least had had to approve Denne's ability to be in the tutoring program.

"*Oui*, Madame," she answered.

Mme Clouet opened a drawer of her desk and gave Denne a copy of the beginning textbook and a stack of vocabulary lists and grammar exercises as well as several dialogues that were to be done orally. She explained that these were just some things that Denne might find useful to review and supplement what Michael would be doing in class.

Denne took the materials and placed them carefully on her stack of books.

"*Merci*, Madame," she replied, and went out into the bustling hallway to make her way toward Room 113, almost numb with panic now that 3:30 had really arrived.

She went to her locker first, to put away the books she didn't need. Crowds of students milled through the hall, slamming locker doors and calling out to each other. There was so much confusion, Denne couldn't even think. She stood for a moment just staring in at the neat stack of new books and her carefully folded gold sweater. Suddenly she had a vision of herself tying the sweater across her shoulders, picking up her books, walking out into the peaceful sunshine and going home to the sanctuary of her own room, where she would lie down on the bed and pull the bright patchwork quilt up over her head.

Instead, her hands cold and her insides shaking, Denne chose the books she needed and moved through the already thinning crowd to Room 113.

The room was empty of people, and when Denne closed the heavy door behind her, it was strangely quiet. She put the materials she was carrying on one of the student desks in the front row and walked over to the window. She looked out unseeingly at the students pouring out of the building and across the lawn. After a minute or two she glanced at her watch and began to walk restlessly around, looking in a desultory way at the globe and the maps on the wall.

She looked at her watch again and, although it only said 3:34, she began to imagine that Michael wasn't coming, that all her agonizing had been for nothing. The thought brought a sharp disappointment. He probably picked up the card saying I was his tutor and decided to forget the whole thing, Denne thought. I always act so stupid when he's around, he probably thinks I'm too dumb to teach him anything!

Just then the door opened swiftly, causing the maps to rattle and flap in the cross-breeze from the windows. Turning quickly, Denne's wide brown eyes looked into Michael's equally wide, even darker brown ones. He stood for a moment just inside the door, smiling at her. She smiled back tentatively, her heart thudding. Neither one moved for a few seconds, and then she realized that she needed to do something. It seemed impossible, since she felt her feet were glued to the floor and her tongue to the roof of her mouth.

"Hi, Denne," Michael said quietly.

Denne swallowed hard and managed to say, "Hi." She tried to add his name, but it just wouldn't come out.

At last she was able to move over to the desk where she'd put the books, and as she sat down in it, Michael turned the one next to it so that they faced each other. He slid into the chair and Denne was suddenly very aware of his nearness. She looked down at the papers in front of her, but all she could see were Michael's long legs in his tight faded jeans and his polished boots.

Michael flipped open a notebook and took a pencil from his shirt pocket. His knit shirt had wide red and blue stripes, but the collar and the trim that held the buttons were white; Denne's eyes strayed to the contrast between the white collar and tan of his neck.

Michael said, "I really appreciate your doing this, Denne. I have to pass an entrance examination in French in order to go to college at McClintock. I've already been offered a football scholarship there, and I really want to go."

Denne was surprised to hear her own voice. "That's O.K. I was looking for a new activity for this year, and my French improved a lot at camp this summer," she said softly.

Denne opened her copy of Michael's textbook. "O.K., now where did you first begin having trouble?" she asked, in what she hoped was a professional-sounding tone.

"I think it was when we first studied irregular verbs," Michael burst out, twisting his pencil in his fingers.

Denne protested. "Michael! Surely not! You had the verb *être* in the very first lesson, and it's irregular."

"Right. Then that was when I started having trouble."

Suddenly all the tension went away and they laughed, their eyes meeting. Michael's teeth were very white against his tanned face, and his brown eyes filled with fun. Denne thought, I can't believe this is really me. I'm sitting here looking into Michael's eyes and we are laughing together! This can't be happening—I'm actually talking to him—we made a joke together!

The tense muscles in her back began to relax and she felt fantastically happy. Shyly, she lowered her eyes.

Michael leaned back in his chair and she looked down at her book. "O.K., Michael, let's do some exercises using *être* and then we'll talk about the conjugations."

Denne loved the sound of the French words, and as she listened to them she became less and less conscious that this was the boy she was afraid to talk to only a few minutes ago. They worked on the exercises for several minutes and then Denne went over the entire present-tense conjugation, going back to the exercises for examples of each form of the verb. Michael really worked and when Denne finally asked him to go through the conjugation alone, he did it without a mistake.

She was elated with the success of her first lesson and with the easy atmosphere between them. "Great, Michael! That's so good; I think you have it now!"

"I think so, too, Denne, and it's all because of you. You are one good teacher!" Michael said fervently. "I never could figure out how that worked, and our class is so big that I hate to keep taking up Madame's time with my questions. I was beginning to wonder whether or not I could ever even learn a foreign language."

"Of course you can! As a matter of fact, I think your accent is quite good," Denne assured him.

His eyes lit up. "You do? You really do?" He gave

her his broadest grin. "Well, then, who knows? I may make it to McClintock yet!"

Denne felt a tremendous burst of joy.

Michael glanced at his watch and said, "Well, teach, you'd better give me my homework assignment because I have to see Coach Hudson at 4:30."

Quickly Denne marked some exercises for Michael to do at home. "We're supposed to meet twice a week, so I'll see you Thursday, O.K.?"

"Right. Thanks again, Denne. See you." Michael stood for a moment just looking at her, then he gathered his books and was gone.

Denne slowly began to stack the teaching materials on top of her notebook. She felt almost dizzy from all the emotions churning around inside of her. She sat still for a minute in the quiet, sunny room going over in her mind every detail of the past few minutes, trying to fit them into her fantasies of who Michael was.

He had seemed genuinely glad that he had learned something about the language, and that surprised her. She'd never thought of him as a serious student. Then she remembered the reason he had given her for being so happy about his progress: he would be able to keep his football scholarship if he could pass the French exam. Face it, Denne, she told herself, he's a good-time, popular guy, just the type for Alicia, interested mainly in football and fun. Maybe he smiled at me and we had a good laugh, but that's all.

She stood up and picked up her books. I need to find a boyfriend who is genuinely into the things that I like, too, she decided as she moved toward the door.

Denne turned off the lights and left the room.

Michael is my student and Alicia's boyfriend, she thought. I'll look for someone more suitable for me. However, as she walked across the empty campus she could see nothing but a tall, blond, brown-eyed boy, his eyes filled with laughter.

Denne stopped for a moment and leaned against the trunk of the maple tree at the end of the walk. The breeze was getting stronger and as the afternoon began to move toward sunset it held a hint of the winter to come. Involuntarily she shivered. She knew that a decision made with her head would not be able to control her heart.

5

"Denne, are you all right? You're just picking at your dinner, and you didn't eat your breakfast." Margaret Drake's blue eyes were clouded with concern. "Did you have any lunch at school, or did you spend the whole time talking to Sharon and ignoring your food?"

Immediately Denne took some green beans onto her fork and ate them. She smiled at her mother reassuringly. "I ate, Mom. It's O.K. I'm just sort of . . . restless, or something."

"Well, you'll be *sick* or something if you don't eat," Margaret replied, with a penetrating glance at her younger daughter.

Denne was glad that just then her father turned the conversation to their plans for the evening, so her mother was distracted. After the meal, while she and her mother cleared the table, she made a special effort to talk and be cheerful and Margaret didn't question her further.

Finally Margaret said, "All right, dear, you've been a big help. Why don't you go on and do your homework now so you won't have to be up late tonight? I know you're tired after all the stress of the first day of school."

Denne wandered out of the kitchen thinking, If you only knew, Mom, if you only knew.

She'd tell her mother about the campaign later, she decided. Right now she couldn't bear to think about it.

She was in no mood to go to her room and study; all the events of the day had created such a turmoil in her mind that she just wanted to go out and lie in the hammock and think. She didn't dare, though; her mother would come out and start talking about homework again for sure.

Slowly Denne climbed the stairs, delaying her arrival at her desk as long as possible. When Alicia called out, Denne welcomed the distraction.

"Denne, is that you? Come here just a minute, O.K.?"

Denne walked to the open door of Alicia's room and stood there for a moment. Alicia was sitting at the dressing table, her back to the door, struggling with the clasp of the gold chain around her neck.

"See if you can fasten this, will you? I can't seem to make it work."

Denne walked over to stand behind her sister, bending her head to look at the tiny fastener. It was just stuck; she moved it a couple of times, inserted the other end of the chain, and closed it.

"There, it's all set. 'Licia, I don't see why you

keep wearing this chain Bob gave you when you go out with Michael."

Alicia shrugged as she picked up her brush and leaned forward to stare intently into wide blue eyes, applying blusher to her fine cheekbones with a practiced hand. She put that brush down and picked up another, smaller one.

"I don't see what difference it makes. It's my chain and I like it."

"Oh, I don't know. It just seems sort of disloyal, or something."

"Oh, good grief, Denne! You're just too young and romantic for your own good! Besides, if it'll make you feel any better, I'm not going out with Michael; I'm going to a cheerleaders meeting at Julie's."

Denne dropped into the pink and yellow armchair under the window. "Ah, yes, romantic! That's the perfect word for me, the belle of Clinton High!"

Alicia finished with the blusher and applied her third coat of mascara. "Well, it's your own fault, Den. I told you to stay in town last summer and try to meet some boys instead of going off to that camp. Last year when I switched over to the Upper Class Building I already had Bob."

"Yes, but you dropped him fast enough when Michael asked you to the Winter Dinner Dance."

"Well, sure." Alicia gave her a mischievous, charming grin. "Who wants to date a basketball player when she can have one of the stars of the football team?"

Denne stared at her sister's face in the lighted mirror and gave her a rueful smile, slowly shaking her head. Alicia looked absolutely perfect and totally natural, as if she hadn't spent the last thirty minutes making up. Her face was faultlessly symmetrical with its enormous dark blue eyes, pert nose and full mouth with pouting lips. She looks like a movie star getting ready for a scene, Denne thought. In fact, she could be *in* a scene right now; this room looks like a set. Margaret and Alicia had worked on the room all summer and it looked like something out of a magazine. One wall was draped with pink and yellow flowered sheets and the dust ruffle and pillow shams on the bed matched them. The comforter and the chair Denne was sitting in were covered with a tiny pink and yellow geometric print, and the curtains and the other walls were solid yellow. Yellow gave Alicia's hair a special glow, and she wore it often.

"Alicia, I don't think it would have made a bit of difference whether I was in town this summer or not; after all, I've been here all my life." Denne twirled a strand of hair thoughtfully. "Sharon says it's determination that makes the difference, and she got asked for a date today."

Alicia began to put a gloss on her lips. "Oh, who asked her?" she muttered, trying not to move her mouth.

"Joe Conley."

"Never heard of him," Alicia declared, putting away the gloss and picking up her hairbrush. "That does have quite a lot to do with it, though, really, Den. Well, now you're just going to have to start going out; Sharon will be busy all the time and you won't have anyone to do things with." She pulled the brush through her long straight hair that shone the color of honey under the light.

"Ho, ho, easier said than done," Denne murmured.

"Let me see what I can do; I'll think about it. . . ."

The phone in the hall shrilled.

"I'll get it," Alicia called, almost to the phone before it could ring again.

Denne sat still, looking around the neat, colorful room, absentmindedly listening to her sister's voice outside the door.

"Hi . . . oh, hi, Julie. I'm wearing jeans, but I'm also wearing my new chenille top, just in case we run into the guys at the Pizza Hut or somewhere. . . . Is Kathy coming, do you know? Oh, well, I should have known she would. . . . I thought maybe they weren't back in town yet. O.K., see you in a few minutes. Bye."

Alicia rushed back to her dressing table, but she didn't sit down. She coiled her hair up quickly and secured it with a large bead-trimmed comb that matched her Indian-beaded belt. She twirled in front of Denne.

"How do I look?"

"Perfect, as usual."

Alicia giggled. "Oh, thanks, Denne." She grabbed her yellow leather clutch bag and hurried toward the door. Then she stopped, came over and ruffled Denne's thick dark curls.

"Don't look so glum, little sister. It'll be all right." She whisked through the door, calling back over her shoulder, "Michael says you're tutoring him. I hope you can help; he really wants that scholarship!" Her steps sounded on the stairs, then the front door slammed.

Denne remained slumped in the cozy chair, idly thinking about Alicia's conversation on the phone. I wonder why she cares whether Kathy is coming, she thought. Kathy Nolan was a senior, too, a cheerleader, almost as pretty and popular as Alicia. For two years Kathy had been dating Brad Fitzgerald, who was captain of the football team. Brad was another one of those dreamy guys, Denne thought. A dreamy guy like Michael. . . .

Finally Denne got up, switched out the light in Alicia's room and went to her own room and to bed. She promised herself that she would get up early in the morning to study; she knew that it was useless to even try that evening. She lay awake for a long time trying to assimilate the events of the day and watching the moving shadows from the big maple tree that the moon was casting onto the wall opposite the foot of her bed.

Denne sat at the lunch table waiting for Sharon to stop talking and finish her lunch.

"Sharon, if you'd hurry up we'd have time to walk around outside a little bit," she complained.

Sharon picked at the cubes of raspberry jello and pretended she hadn't heard. ". . . so not only are we going out for hamburgers tomorrow night after band practice, we actually have a *real* date for the movies on Friday night! Denne, can you believe it? This is still the first week of school and here I am—practically going steady!" Eyes glowing, she looked at Denne and found her staring off into space. Sharon was quiet for a moment, giving Denne a keen glance.

Suddenly she put down her fork, stood and picked up her tray in one swift movement. Denne followed automatically and they put the trays on the conveyor belt, but too late. The warning bell rang as they went toward the outside door. Sighing, they turned toward their lockers instead.

"Want to walk home together? You don't tutor Alicia's big hero today, do you?"

"No, not today. I think there's a French Club meeting, though. Tell you what, why don't you come over to my house later and let me practice my campaign speech on you? Jan and I just finished writing it this morning in government class, and I need all the practice I can get before tomorrow."

Sharon looked embarrassed. "Well, I . . . I'd like to, Denne, but Joe said something about calling me tonight. Who knows, he may get too busy at work and not have time, but I'd hate to be gone if he did call."

Denne looked at Sharon in a puzzled way. "It's O.K., Sharon, I understand." The last bell rang and the girls ran in different directions.

Sharon seems odd, Denne thought. This is weird; there was never any strain between us, but now suddenly there is. She thought about it again occasionally during the afternoon, but most of the time her classes and thoughts of her campaign speech kept her occupied.

Almost before she knew it, school was over for the day and it was time for her French Club meeting. Mme Clouet went to the teachers' lounge for the refreshments she'd brought from home and Denne and Jeff helped rearrange the chairs and tables into a cozy resemblance of a sidewalk cafe.

"That's the fun thing about Madame," Jeff confided as they worked. "She makes everything enjoyable, even class, and especially French Club."

Denne nodded, "I know, and I wish I could relax and enjoy this meeting. I feel so rushed; maybe I've taken on too many projects this year."

"What are you doing that's new?" Jeff looked at Denne with soft gray eyes that were genuinely interested in her answer.

She smiled at him thinking how nice it was to have such a quiet, steady friend. Although they rarely saw each other outside of school, she considered Jeff a good friend, she had thought of him in that way for at least two years now.

"Oh, Jeff, for one thing I let Mr. Walker talk me into running for student council and now I have to make a speech in assembly and everything!" Together they unfolded the white tablecloth from the cabinet and spread it over the long table under the windows. "The saddest thing is—I don't have a prayer of winning. Patty Evans is running against me, so you know what that means."

Jeff shrugged. "Oh, you might be surprised. There may be more people in this school than just me who think that being a cheerleader isn't necessarily a qualification for being elected student council representative."

Denne flashed Jeff a grateful smile and went to help Mme Clouet in the door with the pot of hot chocolate.

As soon as everyone was served hot chocolate and pastries, Madame called the meeting to order.

"Our first order of business is to elect officers. Let's dispense with that, and then we can do the fun things like planning all the parties for the year! Nominations are now open for president."

Jeff's hand shot into the air. "I'd like to nominate Denne Drake," he said firmly.

Denne gasped. "Jeff," she whispered, "I just told you I have too many things to do!"

He grinned mischievously. "But you don't like to do them. I'm trying to get something for you that you'll really enjoy doing."

Before she could protest further, Denne was elected by acclamation.

Mme Clouet smiled happily. "Remember, now, Denne, this makes you a member of the All-School Board. I'll turn your name in to Mr. Monro and he'll send you notices of their meetings. I believe they meet twice a month."

Just what I need, Denne thought. Two more meetings every month!

"It should be a very satisfying job—getting to help make policies and rules for the whole school," Madame teased.

"Right," Denne answered, thinking that that was true, and besides, maybe she'd make some new friends. She relaxed, and really did enjoy the rest of French Club meeting.

That was the last thing she enjoyed for a day or two, however, because before it seemed possible, Thursday morning had come. The day got off to a frustrating start; Denne couldn't get dressed. She had been so busy worrying about what she would say and how she would say it that she had given absolutely no thought to what she would wear for the big campaign speech. She dressed once in a denim skirt and bright plaid shirt, then decided that was too casual. She tried gray corduroy jeans and white cotton sweater, looked in the mirror and said, "Blah. No color; blah." She went to the closet, flipped through everything there in approximately sixty seconds, and didn't see a thing that was even remotely appropriate for standing on stage in front of the entire student body of Clinton High.

Denne's voice cracked with desperation, "Mom," she called, walking to the top of the stairs. "Mom, could you please come up to my room for a minute?"

Margaret's arrival didn't help. Denne still ran from her closet to her mirror to her bureau drawers finding nothing to wear. Finally Margaret picked out an outfit, and Denne put it on forcing herself not to think about whether she was pleased with it. She glanced at her watch as she stepped into the tasseled brown loafers Margaret had set out.

"Mom, will you drive me, please? I've spent so much time with this I'm going to be late if I walk."

"I will if you promise to calm down on the way," her mother replied with a sympathetic smile.

6

Even her mom's supportive company didn't help, though, and when Denne got out of the car in front of the school she was so nervous that she wished she could walk right in to the auditorium, give her speech and be done with it that minute. Instead, she had to suffer until third hour.

She went into Mrs. Henderson's homeroom just as the last bell was ringing, and as she walked to her seat in front of everyone she was suddenly conscious of what she was wearing. Margaret had chosen a gold corduroy skirt and blazer, and a plain white shirt with a black ribbon at the neck. Denne suddenly felt blah again, blah and dowdy and miserable.

She got through the first classes of the morning in a trance. When the bell rang for third hour she went directly backstage and joined the candidates who were being briefed by Mr. Monro, the assistant principal.

"All of you will sit in the chairs which have been placed in a semicircle at the sides of the stage. After my opening remarks, the two candidates for junior representative will come forward and make their speeches; Denne, you first, since we're using alphabetical order. Then we'll have the speeches from the candidates for senior representative; then the students will cast their ballots as they leave the auditorium. Each class has two representatives on the council who were chosen before the close of school last year, so this election will complete the process, and Mr. Walker and the council will be able to get right to work."

Denne grasped most of what Mr. Monro was saying, but her real concentration was on Patty Evans.

Patty was in a sophisticated black suit with a straight skirt and fitted jacket. She was wearing a blue silk blouse that was exactly the color of her eyes and high-heeled black sandals with ankle straps. Her smile was bright and she was fairly bubbling with personality, as usual. Denne felt plain and she wished desperately that there were some way she could gracefully get out of the whole situation before they left the protection of the wings. It was too late, though; Mr. Monro was leading the way onto the stage. Denne followed close behind on shaking legs.

The opening remarks seemed to take only seconds; then Mr. Monro was calling Denne's name and there was polite applause as she came to the podium. She glanced nervously at the note cards in her hand, although she had practiced the speech so many times that she would probably still know it by memory when she was an old woman, she thought.

At first her voice wouldn't come out, and when it did it sounded different to Denne, almost as if it belonged to someone else. The speech seemed to belong to someone else, too; she couldn't keep her mind on the ideas in it; she just read mechanically and tried not to think about how many people were out there listening to her and looking at her. She went through the cards very quickly and long before the allotted ten minutes had passed she was saying, ". . . so if we have a school-wide book fair to benefit both the library and the campus beautification projects, we will all have the satisfaction of knowing that we have made lasting contributions to Clinton High."

There was polite applause and Denne sat down. Her only feeling was relief at being able to blend into the background. She savored that feeling for a moment, and then began to concentrate on Patty, who was being greeted with enthusiastic applause as she strolled to the microphone on her high heels. Patty began her speech with a joke, and then got to the main point of her campaign.

"I think that school should be fun as well as educational, and that one of the most important things a student council can do is to promote school spirit. So, if I am elected junior representative, I am going to advocate school sponsored parties for each of the major holidays each year and a school dance once each month."

Wild whistling and cheering greeted this statement and Patty had to wait several minutes before she could go on. She stood gracefully at the speaker's stand, one arm leaning on it slightly, her blue eyes sparkling out at the applauding students. She loves all that, Denne thought; she is perfectly at home in the midst of so much attention. Denne's heart sank.

How could I ever begin to compete with someone like that? she asked herself. There she is, so poised and so beautiful, dressed in the very latest popular style and all the other kids love her. Oh, I wish I could get off this stage—I wish I had alienated Mr. Walker forever before I gave in and got myself into this humiliating mess! How could I have been so stupid?

As Patty continued painting a glowing picture of Clinton High as it would be if she were elected to the student council, Denne berated herself, too, for having run on such a dull platform as improving the library and the campus grounds. Patty finished her speech to more wild applause and whistles and walked calmly back to her chair. She crossed her legs and sat smiling out at the crowd, her hair gleaming in the stage lights.

Denne didn't know how she sat through the two seniors' speeches, but she did, and when the candidates were finally dismissed and the balloting began, she quickly left the auditorium and went back to government class. She opened a book and pretended to read, trying not to be noticed as the other students began trickling back into the room. A few people spoke to her, but no one mentioned the speech or the campaign except for Jan, who slid into her chair next to Denne's and said, "You did fine, Denne; that was a good speech we wrote!"

Mr. Walker came in about that time and before he started class he, too, commented, but not very enthusiastically, "Denne, you gave a good speech. Thanks."

At lunch Sharon told Denne she'd done well, and Jeff mentioned it in French, but they were the only ones all day long who brought the subject up to Denne. She decided that her performance had been too embarrassing to talk about, and she went to her classes in a fog of depression. By 3:30, when it was time to tutor Michael, she felt she was the most boring, ineffectual person in the world.

This time he was early, waiting for Denne with the desks already turned to face each other. He gave her a big smile.

"You'll be proud of me; I've really done my homework and I can conjugate two more verbs: *aller* and *avoir!*"

Denne sat down and opened her book without a word.

"Hey, now, Denne, what's wrong? Where's your smile today?" Michael's tone was teasing. Denne's throat was tight and she couldn't answer, but she glanced at him and then looked back at the book.

"Oh, don't be angry with me, please, teacher, I did all my work and I got to class on time," he bantered.

Denne looked at Michael and tried to smile, but her lips quivered and tears came to her eyes.

Michael's mood changed abruptly. He leaned toward her, concern in his dark eyes and in his voice.

"Oh, Denne, don't cry. What is it? What has made you so unhappy?"

The caring way Michael spoke to her and the sense of his nearness gave Denne a sudden desire to lay her head on his broad chest and just forget the whole world existed. She continued looking into his eyes that seemed almost black now with worry; she couldn't have pulled her gaze away if she'd tried.

He frowned. "O.K., tell me. What's wrong?"

Denne burst out, "Oh, it's just that I made such a fool of myself today in assembly. I gave a stupid speech and I looked stupid, and I should never have been there in the first place!" Denne heard the words coming out of her mouth with a sense of disbelief. How could she possibly be talking to Michael—Michael, of all people—about her personal feelings? The words kept pouring out of their own volition; she had no control over her mouth.

"I am not in the same league with girls like Patty Evans and I ought to know that and keep myself out of situations like that one today."

Michael leaned back in his chair and smiled at her. "Denne, listen to me. You're *not* in the same league with Patty, true. You are much superior to her. You remember that." He looked into Denne's eyes as if he would read her thoughts.

She felt a shock of cold surprise that quickly turned to a warmth that spread through her entire body. She couldn't say a word; she just kept staring at Michael.

"The student council election at this school is a popularity contest, that's all. There were some good ideas in your speech and it isn't your fault if the students didn't respond to them."

Denne managed a smile.

"There, that's better," Michael grinned. "Now, let's get on to the lesson; I can't wait to show off my new knowledge."

Michael had, indeed, been studying, and once Denne got into the French lesson she forgot all about everything else. Everything else, that is, except the tall boy across from her. No matter how absorbed she was, she was always aware of his strong hands on the desk so near hers and his brown eyes that were on hers every time she glanced up at him.

The hour was over far too soon. While Michael gathered his books Denne tore a sheet from her small notebook and quickly jotted down his assignment for next time. He stood, his books under his arm, waiting for her to finish. When she did, she looked up, holding the little piece of paper out to Michael. He was looking down at her with an expression she couldn't quite understand, and when he took the paper his hard brown fingers touched hers. A thrill went through her.

"Thanks, Denne," he smiled. "Now you remember what I told you and don't worry any more, O.K.?"

She nodded. "O.K.," she agreed, softly.

"Fine. See you Monday," he called as he left the room.

Denne walked all the way home still feeling Michael's touch on her fingers. She kept hearing his voice, so full of concern for her feelings, saying, "You are much superior to her." Over and over she thought about the look in his eyes as he leaned toward her across the desk. How would she ever be able to think about anything else, ever again?

But how could she let herself keep thinking about him this way? After all, she told herself, this is my sister's boyfriend. He'd never give her up for me, and even if, by some miracle, he did, I'd feel terribly guilty. Oh, the whole idea is just ridiculous! she thought.

When Denne got home no one else was there;

even Muffin was asleep. She didn't even go to the kitchen for a snack, she went straight to her room, dropped her books and jacket in a heap on the desk, kicked her shoes toward the closet, and stretched out across the patchwork crazy quilt.

She lay on her back, watching the leaves of the maple tree out the window and, in spite of the lecture she'd just given herself, she began to replay in her mind the entire hour with Michael, minute by minute. She was just reaching the end of it, his fingers touching hers (she could actually feel the warmth again) when the phone shrilled in the hallway.

Michael's voice came from the receiver and it was like a part of her daydream; it was as if her thoughts had been so strong that they had drawn him to call her.

"Denne? It's Michael."

"Hello," she managed.

"How are you, feeling better now?"

"Yes, Michael, thanks. I . . . I've almost forgotten the whole thing."

"Great, that's the way to go. Listen, Denne, is Alicia around? I need to talk to her."

Denne froze. Alicia? Alicia? Of course, you idiot, she told herself. After all, he *is* Alicia's boyfriend. Your sister, you do remember your sister, the popular Alicia.

"Uh . . . she's not here right now."

"O.K., thanks. I'll try Julie's house—I really need to talk with her right away. See you, Denne."

"Yeah, see you," she muttered, almost missing the phone as she put the receiver back into place.

Denne rushed back into her room, ripping off the blouse and skirt, looking for her jeans and T-shirt.

She had to get out of the house and do something. Something physical, something hard that would work all the tension out of her.

She dressed and found her tennis racquet. I'll call Sharon, she thought, and see if she wants to play a quick game. She was standing in the hall with the receiver at her ear when she remembered that Sharon was with Joe, this afternoon, and this evening, and they had a date tomorrow night.

Feeling completely alone, she put the phone back and walked slowly down the stairs, tapping her racquet against her leg.

7

Denne went into homeroom Monday morning with only one thought: get the announcement of election winners over with and forget the whole affair as quickly as possible. All weekend she had dreaded this second public humiliation. It won't be as long as my speech was, and the whole student body won't be there, but it's going to be embarrassing just the same, she thought. Patty Evans with her silly speech is going to beat me.

It'll be another occasion for everyone to compare me with Alicia, too, she mused as Mrs. Henderson began reading the announcements. When she ran for student council, from Mr. Walker's homeroom, she won. I wonder what he'll say to me when I walk into class today. I'll bet he wishes he'd never suggested that I try for the office.

At last the routine announcements were finished

and Mrs. Henderson's voice cut into Denne's thoughts.

"I'm sure you're all waiting for the results of the student council election," she said. "I have them right here. Senior Representative is Tom Cawthon, Junior Representative is Patty Evans. . . ."

Her voice went on, but Denne didn't hear anything else. Even though she had been expecting to lose, the actual public acknowledgment of that fact caused her to turn cold inside and warm on the outside. She felt her cheeks flush red and she was afraid to look up from her penciled doodling for fear that forty pairs of eyes would be staring at her. Why can't I learn just to stay in my place? she berated herself. I am good at my studies and that is all. I need to learn that I can't compete with beautiful, popular girls like Patty and Alicia in anything: not in school government, not in activities, and most of all, not in dating. The sooner I accept that, the better off I'll be.

The thought was like a weight inside her as she rose from her seat and began making her way out of the room when the bell rang. One or two students muttered "Sorry, Denne," as they moved out into the hallway, but that was all, and for most of the morning Denne was allowed to fade into the woodwork.

Then she went to government class and Jan started talking about the election as soon as she saw Denne.

"Denne, don't worry. You did a very good job with the speech."

"Thanks, Jan. I appreciate your helping me write it."

"This student body just isn't ready for anything as mature as helping to buy books for the library. All they can think about is parties and fun," Jan declared as she opened her notebook and placed her books under her desk. "I just think it's sad when all they can think about in an election is popularity."

Denne didn't quite know how she could answer that, and the slight pause made Jan think about how her remark sounded. She blushed painfully.

"I . . . I didn't mean that you aren't popular, Denne, I . . ."

Denne nodded. "I know, Jan; it's O.K. We did the best that we could with the campaign, and now it's over and I'd like to just forget about it."

Jan nodded as Mr. Walker began class.

"We are going to form study groups today and begin work on a series of oral reports that will be due next week; the first ones to be given on Monday. You will choose a chairman for each group who will coordinate the work and organize the oral presentations. I'll bring you a list of topics to be covered after you are in your groups."

The second Mr. Walker stopped talking Jan leaned across to Denne. "Let's be in the same group, O.K.?" she whispered anxiously.

Denne was a little puzzled, but she didn't really care whose group she was in, and she answered, "O.K."

Jan stayed close by her side as they joined the rest of the class in breaking up the rows of chairs into small circles and dividing themselves into groups of five. Once they were settled with three other girls, Jan took charge.

"Let's have Denne be chairman, O.K.? Is that all right with everyone?" she asked, her straight light brown hair swinging across her face. She brushed it back and looked around the group, her hazel eyes intent. "Would you like to do that, Denne?"

Denne was so tired and bruised from all the doubts about herself that had been filling her mind these past few days that she never wanted to try to be a leader in anything ever again. Not even in something as small as a study group.

She raised her eyes to say no, but Jan was looking at her so eagerly she knew there would be an argument if she refused. For just a minute Denne looked into Jan's narrow hazel eyes under her straight brows. What is she trying to do, anyway? Denne asked herself. Why does she keep pushing me? Jan's eyes told her nothing.

Finally Denne shrugged and said, "O.K., I'll do it if nobody else wants to."

Everyone settled down to look at the list Mr. Walker brought them.

They worked steadily for most of the hour, then a few minutes before the bell rang Mr. Walker told them they could have the remainder of the time to relax. The other three girls in the group were talking among themselves and Jan turned to Denne again.

"Did you have a good weekend? Did your family go someplace?" she asked.

"No, we were home most of the time," Denne answered, "why?"

"Oh, I tried to call you a couple of times, but no one answered and I decided you must be out of town."

"You must have just missed us," Denne said, surprised that Jan had called. "Did you want to tell me something important?"

"No, I thought we might get together; I was just looking for something to do," Jan smiled.

The bell rang and the students began moving the chairs back into straight rows. Denne thought about the lonely weekend she had just had; Alicia had been with Michael, of course, and Sharon with Joe, and she had wandered around by herself unable to really concentrate or get interested in much of anything. Mostly she had compared herself with girls like Patty Evans and Alicia and wished she had never left her room to go to school in the first place. Another weekend like that would drive her crazy.

Denne looked at Jan, stacking her books on her arm. She's probably just trying to be friendly, she thought. Sounds like she was as bored as I was last weekend. Impulsively, she spoke.

"Jan, why don't you come over to my house this Friday night? We'll listen to records and make pizza or something."

Jan's face lit up. "I'd love to, Denne. That's a great idea."

Denne walked out of class with Jan thinking, Well, at least I'm learning to make new friends. I certainly can't sit around all the time and wait for Sharon to be free.

At her locker Jan suddenly turned to Denne with a pained look on her face. "Oh, Denne, I'm so sorry—I just remembered that I'm going out of town with my mother this weekend." Jan was so frustrated she slapped her forehead. "Oh, no! I really wanted to come over!"

"Don't be upset; that's all right. You can come over the next Friday. A week from Friday night; we'll make definite plans right now. We'll just put it off a week, that's all."

Jan hugged her gratefully. "Great, Denne. That's perfect. I just forgot about the trip when we were planning for this Friday, and I know there's absolutely no way I can talk my mother into letting me stay here." She put away her books with a happy flourish. "O.K., a week from Friday it is," she called as Denne left her.

Denne wondered whether it would be fun for Jan to come over. They hardly knew each other and had nothing in common except the brief, ill-fated campaign. Still, it was nice to have some plans and a semblance of a social life.

Denne was doubly glad to have a new friendship beginning after she met Sharon for lunch. They sat, picking at their food, glancing politely at each other as if they had just met. It was driving Denne crazy.

"Sharon, what in the world is wrong with you? You, the mouth, are not saying a word. I can't believe it."

Shrugging, Sharon blushed slightly and said, "Oh, I don't know. I . . . I just don't have anything to say, I guess."

Try as she would, Denne could never get anymore out of Sharon than that, and she walked to class with a terrible empty feeling inside. It was as if an important part of her life were dying and she couldn't do a thing to stop it, since she didn't even know what was causing it. She kept thinking about Sharon all afternoon; how close they had always been, how much fun they'd had as best friends since the fourth grade, how strange it seemed to feel any kind of awkwardness between them, especially this wall that seemed to have appeared overnight.

By the time she got to French class, Denne was really depressed over the state of her friendship with

Sharon, and was glad to find Jeff waiting for her just outside the door with his usual calm smile.

"See, what did I tell you?" she greeted him. "You *are* the only person in this school who thinks cheerleading is not a qualification for student council representative."

Jeff laughed. "Maybe so. But you don't need that anyway, Denne; you have too many other, more interesting activities, thanks to loyal admirers like me."

"Oh, yes, loyal admirers like you have trapped me into more meetings than I have time to attend and terrible, wrenching decisions about how the school should be run!" she answered, as they went into class and took their seats.

French class was fun, as usual, and Jeff and Denne had a good time until the last five minutes of class when Madame tapped on her desk.

"I want to announce that there will be a quiz on Monday; one week from today. It will be a review quiz over the literature that you studied last year, and it will also cover the two stories we have read this year. Please be prepared."

Jeff grasped Denne's hand in mock dismay. "Oh, no! What will we do? How can we prepare for such a thing?"

Madame's words penetrated Denne's consciousness. "Really, Jeff, this isn't very funny. Did you hear her? This will cover what we studied last year. How much do you remember about the literature we read last year? We have one week to get ready, and you know how hard her tests always are!" Denne felt a rising panic. She was the star of this class; her performance in French was a big source of pride to her, her one sure source of confidence. It would be severely damaged if she made a low grade on an important quiz.

She clung to Jeff's hand desperately. "We have to get together and study. We can each go over half the stories from last year and then tell them to each other. As soon as we start talking about them we'll probably remember a lot of things."

Jeff reddened slightly as Denne leaned close to him imploringly. "R-right," he stuttered. "W-we could cover the material much faster that way."

"O.K., Jeff, I'll tell you what we should do. We'll study individually this week, then Friday night let's get together and go over everything. Is that all right with you? Can you come over to my house?"

Jeff looked pleased and embarrassed and nervous and happy all at the same time. "I . . . I think so. Yeah, I'm sure I can."

The bell rang and the other students left the classroom, but Denne and Jeff stayed for a few minutes to decide which stories each would study during the week. They did so quickly, and Denne looked at her watch.

"Oh, my student is waiting. I have to run." She closed and stacked her books and stood up all in one quick motion.

"See you tomorrow, Jeff," she said, going toward the door.

"Uh . . . yeah," he answered slowly.

Denne glanced back as she left the room; Jeff was sitting in his desk, not moving, following her intently with his clear warm, gray eyes.

8

Friday night, as she brought her books downstairs, Denne tried to decide on the best room for the study session. Her parents were watching television in the den, and the living room didn't have a table good for studying, so she went through the kitchen to the little room on the back of the house that everyone called the sun porch. It had windows all around, and in the daytime it always seemed flooded with sunlight. Tonight it was private and inviting, the windows covered with basket weave curtains that matched the off-white walls, Margaret's plants giving a touch of the green outdoors in corners and hanging from the ceiling. The room was so cozy that Denne had a sudden, sharp wish that it was Michael who would be sharing it with her that evening.

As soon as the thought came she realized how much she had been wanting to be with him all week.

Both times that she had tutored him he had been in a hurry to finish and get to football practice and she hadn't had a chance to talk with him about anything personal. Sharon was becoming more and more distant and Denne had a feeling that if she could talk it over with him it might help; after all, it had made her feel much better to talk with him about her disastrous campaign speech. Just thinking about the caring in his voice and in his eyes that day made her want to spend the evening daydreaming about him instead of studying with Jeff.

That would be brilliant, she told herself sarcastically. Then maybe he'd call up on the phone and ask for Alicia. No, he wouldn't—he is out with Alicia at this very moment.

Sighing, Denne put her books on a chair and, moving a big potted fern from the corner table to the floor, she began pulling the table to the center of the room. She moved two of the floral-covered chairs over to the table and arranged the lamps so that the light would fall over their shoulders onto their books. She stacked her dictionary and last year's notebooks in the middle and checked to make sure she had clean paper and a couple of pens.

Just then the doorbell rang. She heard her mother's footsteps going to the door and then her voice. "Denne," she called, "Jeff is here."

Denne met Jeff in the hallway and led him back to the sun porch, taking the large bottle of Coke he'd brought.

"I thought it would be a good idea to work out here so we'd be close to the kitchen for snacks," she joked, as he put his books and notebooks on the table.

Jeff smiled a little shyly and ran his hand through his hair. "Who knows, we might even do a little French cooking," he answered, his voice stiff.

Denne got ice and glasses and poured the Coke. When she took the full glasses out to the table she saw that Jeff had already opened his book to last year's first French story and that he was arranging the notes he'd made about it beside the book.

"You are doubtless the most efficient study partner anyone ever had," she teased. "We'll make all the points on the stories you've prepared, at least."

Jeff grinned, and as they got into the French he completely relaxed and things got back to normal. They reviewed six stories; then Denne called for a break.

"Au secours! J'en ai assez!" She pleaded pathetically, her hands folded in front of her.

Jeff chuckled and shook his head. He turned the page to the next story and, giving her the title, asked for a plot summary. She attacked, snatching his book from him and pretending to beat him with it. Laughing, he ducked and tried to ward off the blows with upraised arms, then he went on the offensive and took the book away from Denne, holding her arm still with one of his large hands.

"Come on, let's get something to eat and forget this nonsense about quizzes and books," Denne said, taking Jeff's hand and pulling him to his feet.

"O.K., but I'm too tired to do any fancy cooking," he answered, letting her lead him into the kitchen.

Jeff dumped chips into a bowl while Denne took two kinds of dip and ham and cheese for sandwiches out of the refrigerator.

Jeff turned from the counter at the same time Denne closed the refrigerator door and faced him.

"Denne . . ." he said, unexpected tension in his voice. "Denne, this has really been fun. We should . . . uh . . . would you like. . . ."

The change in Jeff's tone and the uneasiness that was suddenly between them fell together in Denne's mind and fit with an intuitive feeling that she'd had all week but had never taken time to think through or put into words. Instinctively, she was certain that Jeff was about to ask her for a date.

"You're right—we should do this more often. It's the only way to really go over a lot of material in a short time, and it's a lot more fun than studying alone. I think we should make it a practice this year; every time Madame assigns an cxam, we'll get together and prepare for it," she babbled, trying to stay in control of the conversation.

Jeff didn't push it; he looked a bit disappointed, but he agreed to the long-term study plan and helped Denne make the sandwiches and carry the food out to the sun porch table, talking casually about French Club and music and whether he should try out for basketball when the season came.

They never got back to really studying any more, and around 10:00 Jeff left. Denne walked with him to the front door and took his jacket from the hall closet. He put it on and standing in the open doorway he looked down at Denne with the same clear gaze she'd seen at school the day they'd made plans for this evening.

"Denne, I have really enjoyed this," he said, his voice full of feeling. He looked into her eyes for a minute more, then turned and loped down the steps and onto the walk.

Denne closed the door and went back to the sun porch to clear things away. There was a kind of low-keyed confusion of emotions swirling in the pit of her stomach.

She carried the leftovers and dishes into the kitchen and put them away, berating herself for being so stupid. I have been wanting a boyfriend, she thought, and now I know that Jeff wants to date me. He is a good friend and we have fun together, and I should have let him ask me out.

She closed and stacked her books and papers and put them on the arm of the long rattan sofa that sat under the windows. She put the lamp back in place and went over to move the chairs. Her hands on the back of one of them, she stood very still as the realization came. I will never be able to think of Jeff as a boyfriend, she thought. He is my friend and being with him is almost like having a brother, but I didn't let him ask me out because I will never feel any other way about him. He's held my hand and we've scuffled around, and I've taken his hand and there's never been that warm flash of magic that was there when. . . .

She stared unseeingly at the eggshell-colored wall. The thought of Michael's touch actually made her fingers tingle again with the thrill she had felt when his fingers had barely brushed hers. The warmth spread through her whole body as she thought of the look in his brown eyes when he was so concerned about her feelings and in his voice as he leaned toward her saying, "You are much superior. . . ." Denne stood without moving, reliving those wonderful moments for the thousandth time.

Finally she shook herself back to reality and continued putting the room in order. She replaced the chairs in their corners, knowing she'd done the right thing with Jeff. There's no point in starting a dating relationship with him, she affirmed. In the end, he would just get hurt, and I like him too much to ever want to hurt him.

She replaced the table and, standing in the doorway, glanced around the room to make sure it was back to normal. Noticing her books, she picked them up and went out, climbing the stairs very slowly.

In her room, getting into her sleep-shirt, though, the realistic part of her attacked that attitude. I've always been scared of a boy-girl relationship, she thought. It's just as I told Sharon the other day; I simply cannot talk to boys and flirt and act like a girl with them, and maybe I'm afraid to try, even with someone I know as well as Jeff. I'm just not letting myself get a boyfriend because I wouldn't know what to do with one. All that about Michael is just an excuse; he doesn't know I'm alive except as Alicia's little sister and as his French tutor. *He* certainly doesn't know there's any excitement when our fingers touch.

She wandered restlessly to her desk and restacked the books on it, then went to the bureau and fiddled with the comb, brush and knickknacks on top of it. I ought to date Jeff, she told herself. At least maybe I would gain some self-confidence that I could use when I do meet someone magic I could date. And it would make Sharon happy, she thought. She wanted us both to have boyfriends and double-date, and then we'd have lots to talk about.

Denne stood perfectly still. That's the problem! That's what's wrong with Sharon! We can't talk to each other because all she wants to talk about is Joe and their dates and I'm not dating anyone, and she doesn't want to make me feel bad! She's acting weird because she doesn't want to hurt my feelings!

Happiness and relief flooded through Denne. She glanced at the clock with the idea of calling Sharon, but it said 10:45. She probably isn't home yet, and I don't want to wake her parents, she thought.

Denne got into bed, snuggled into the pillow and relaxed, secure in the thought that her friendship with Sharon would soon be back to its old warmth and closeness. I know she would agree that I should get experience to use later on with someone magic, she reflected. As she drifted off to sleep the phrase "someone magic" revolved around and around in her head, and with it the image of a tall brown-eyed boy with shining blond hair and an enchanting smile.

9

Well, Denne, are you ready for the big quiz?"

Denne looked up from her combination lock to find Jeff smiling down at her. She smiled back.

"I'll never be ready for this one, but I'm a lot closer to it after Friday night. That really helped, and I studied quite a bit more yesterday afternoon."

She took the books she needed from the locker and closed the lock again.

"What class do you have now?" Jeff asked.

"Mr. Walker's. Where are you going?"

"Mrs. Ulrich's. I'll walk down that way with you, O.K.?"

"Sure. On the way you can even tell me some of the finer points about the masterpieces of French literature."

As they passed the door to Mr. Sampson's room, it opened suddenly and a crowd of students poured out, almost late to their next classes because of their overenthusiastic teacher. Jeff took Denne's elbow and pulled her closer to him to guide her through the milling group. Just as they came out of it into a relatively clear space in the hallway, they came face to face with Michael, and his fellow football player, Brad Fitzgerald. They stopped suddenly, to keep from bumping into each other, and Michael stood for a second looking at Denne, and then at Jeff, several reactions flitting across his face in rapid succession.

Denne was in no condition to read his thoughts; she was startled to see him, and the old panicky feeling of excitement came back to her in full force. She couldn't take her eyes from his at first, then once she looked away she couldn't look directly at him again.

"Oh, hi, Denne," he said casually.

"Hi," she managed to answer.

"See you this afternoon," he called, as he and Brad moved around Denne and Jeff and went down the hall.

Jeff was still holding Denne's elbow. "What was that all about?" he asked.

"Oh, he's my student, you know, he's the one I tutor in French twice a week," she answered, moving away from Jeff's hand. "We'd better hurry or we're going to be late for both our classes."

Jeff left Denne at the door of government class and rushed for Mrs. Ulrich's classroom just as the last bell rang.

Jan was helping some other students pull the chairs into circles for the study groups, and when she saw Denne come in she motioned eagerly for her to join them.

Mr. Walker started talking as Denne sat down.

"I'm going to put you on your honor to go ahead with your group work this morning; I have a meeting in the main office. Mr. Monro will look in on you from time to time, and I'm sure I'll be back before the hour is up."

Denne's group worked for about half the hour, then they gradually degenerated into just sitting around and talking. Jan could think of nothing else but Friday night.

"I know it's going to be so much fun," she prattled, "but I've thought of another idea. Why don't we make it an overnighter? We could go to a movie and then go to your house and make pizza and then sit up and talk all night!" Her eyes, filled with enthusiasm, were fixed on Denne's. Denne was surprised that Jan would invite herself to stay overnight and she wondered what in the world they would have to talk about if they did stay awake the whole time, but she didn't know how to say no.

"I guess so. What's on at the movies?"

"Oh, I don't know. We'll just have to check and see. I'll find out and tell you tomorrow."

Just then, Mr. Walker came back in and made the assignment for next time. Denne heard the last part of it.

". . . so be ready tomorrow to give the first section of your oral report to the class. You'll be graded on how well you present the material in addition to how well you have prepared it."

After class Jan waited to talk to Mr. Walker about her oral presentation, and as Denne walked by on her way out of the room she touched her arm.

"I'll tell you all the movies tomorrow, and we can choose the one we want," she told her.

"O.K., Jan, fine," Denne answered. As she went out into the hallway she wondered how a visit to her house could ever live up to the anticipation Jan was generating around it.

She didn't have time to think about it now, though, Denne wanted every spare minute and every bit of energy to finish preparing for the French quiz. She decided to take her lunch hour to study, so when it began she went to her locker for her French books and then ran into the cafeteria. Sharon was already standing in line.

"I'm going to the library to study for my French quiz, Sharon," she announced breathlessly, "but I really need to talk to you. Can you meet me at The School Store after band practice?"

Surprised, Sharon agreed. "Why, yeah, sure."

"O.K., see you then," Denne threw back over her shoulder.

She worked in the library during lunch, then kept the French books with her and peeked into them and at her notes every chance she got during her afternoon classes. By the time she arrived in French class her nerves were jangling and she felt sure that she was about to lose her one source of self-confidence by disgracing herself with a D on the test.

Madame passed out the quiz papers, Denne looked hers over, and sighed with relief. There was only one question that she wasn't sure of, and she thought she could at least salvage a part of it. She wrote steadily all hour and finished only a minute ahead of the bell.

After class Jeff wanted to talk about the test, but Denne just wanted to celebrate the fact that it was over by seeing Michael as soon as possible. Ever since she'd seen him that morning he had been hovering in the back of her mind again.

"I missed that one question about *Le Misanthrope,*" Jeff complained.

"I only got part of it, but the rest was easy, didn't you think?" she asked him as she stacked her books and took her sweater from the back of the chair. "See you tomorrow, Jeff."

"O.K., bye, Denne."

When Denne got to the assigned room, Michael wasn't there. She moved their chairs into the accustomed places and sat down, but she didn't open a book. She was tired of French and of studying, and all she wanted to do was stare at the streak of sunlight coming in at the windows and think about how it would look shining on Michael's yellow hair.

Michael was almost ten minutes late, and his first words ruined Denne's mood completely. "Your sister is hard to get away from; I've been telling her over and over again that I had to be here at 3:30, but she wouldn't stop talking. Thanks for waiting, Denne."

Denne got through the exercises somehow, depressed at the very thought of Alicia and Michael so deep in conversation that they couldn't tear themselves away. As usual, Michael had studied and he did well, so she added an extra assignment to the list she had prepared. He stood beside her chair, in a hurry to get to football practice, waiting for her to finish writing. Suddenly he spoke.

"Who was that guy you were with this morning?"

Surprised, Denne glanced up into Michael's brown eyes. There was a new expression in them, but she didn't know what it was.

"Jeff Watson."

"Are you dating him or what?" he asked.

The mere suggestion that Michael had thought of her in connection with a date was enough to make Denne's hands shake a little.

"No, he's in my French, class; we've been friends for a long time," she answered.

He took the assignment sheet and was gone without another word.

All the way to The School Store Denne wondered about those questions. Michael had never seemed particularly interested in anything about her life outside of her abilities in French, she thought. Why this sudden interest in who she was walking around with?

Sharon was waiting in a booth toward the back of the popular hangout where the noise from the jukebox wasn't quite so loud. She smiled when Denne slid into the seat across from her, and looked really glad to see her. It's almost like old times already, Denne thought.

"Hi, Sharon. How was band practice?"

"Fine, how was the French quiz?"

"I did O.K.; wasted a lot of time studying too hard."

The waitress appeared, pad and pencil in hand.

"Two Cokes," Sharon said, and the girl went away again.

Denne took a deep breath. "Sharon, I want to tell you that any time you want to talk about Joe, that's fine. I'd like to listen. I've decided that you haven't been talking about him or your dates because I'm not dating and I don't have any one to talk about, too," she said, all in a rush.

Sharon's freckled face was surprised; her blue eyes

were warm, smiling at Denne. "Well, I *was* sort of wishing that we could share stories—I hate to do all the talking."

Denne laughed. "No, you don't. You've done all the talking many, many times and it never bothered you a bit. You just don't want to talk about all your fascinating romantic adventures and make me feel like the spinster of the week!"

Sharon grinned. "Oh, I suppose you're right." She began to tear the wrapper off her straw as soon as the waitress set a Coke in front of each of them. She went on, "Really, Denne, the whole problem would be solved if you'd cooperate with my plans for our double dates." She sipped her Coke, looking over at Denne with her eyes wide. "Just think what fun it would be to rehash the whole evening together!"

Denne sighed. "It really would be, Sharon. But it seems that we lack one essential ingredient for that little scenario: another boy." She tapped the tabletop with her still unopened straw.

"I thought the other day we might have a candidate for the position, but I was wrong," she said casually.

Sharon got so excited she almost choked. "*Who?* Who was it? Denne, tell me right now! And why did you decide it wouldn't work, you foolish girl?"

"Jeff Watson. I think he was trying to ask me for a date, but I wouldn't let him."

"You wouldn't let him!" Sharon sputtered. "Denne, you had a perfect chance to fulfill my prophecy and you blew it!" She pounded on the table in frustration. "O.K., I want every last detail!" she stated firmly.

Denne replayed the evening with Jeff for Sharon,

wondering again as she did so whether she had made a mistake in not encouraging him.

Sharon thought she had. "Oh, Denne, you might really enjoy going out with him. Why didn't you?"

"Well, for one thing, I am panicked to think of how stupid I would probably act on a date and that would mess up the friendship we have now; and for another thing, I just don't think I can ever. . . ." She wanted to say "feel the way I do about Michael" but she still couldn't talk about that with any one. Instead, she said, "think of him as anything but a friend."

Sharon was determined. "Well, so what? What harm would it do for you to go out with him anyway?"

"It would hurt him, Sharon. I think he really likes me, and if I could never feel the same way about him. . . ." Denne's voice trailed off as she was lost again in her own thoughts.

"All right, all right; so Jeff isn't a good idea. But how about somebody else? I could ask Joe if he has any friends who aren't dating anyone right now." Sharon sat up straight and beamed as an idea hit her. "I know!" she crowed. "Joe has a cousin, Reece, over in Lewisville who just broke up with his girl friend! Why didn't I think of that sooner? I haven't met him, but I'm sure he's very nice. Of course, it's perfect! Let me try to arrange something for this weekend, O.K.?"

Denne was astonished by Sharon's swift take-over. "I . . . I can't this weekend, Sharon. I've invited Jan Little over for Friday evening, and she's invited herself to make it an overnighter, and Saturday I'll probably be really tired." She hastily drained her Coke cup. "Anyway, I don't think I'd like a blind date. You know that they never work."

"That isn't necessarily so!" Sharon replied indignantly. "You and Reece might really have a good time."

Denne threw her sweater around her shoulders and gathered up her books. "We might, but I very strongly doubt it. Come on, Sharon, we'd better go; it's getting late."

The girls walked slowly together to the corner where they always parted, chatting about happenings in the band, French club activities and Joe. As they said good-bye, Sharon stated flatly, "I'm not going to give up on you and Reece, Denne. I still think that's one of the best ideas I've had in a long time." She walked away before Denne could formulate another protest.

10

Denne walked the rest of the way slowly, thoughts of Jeff and the unknown Reece floating around in her head. Maybe I should date one of them, she decided; that might help get Michael out of my system. The magic name evoked all of the old feelings, and as she climbed the front steps Denne was wondering again why Michael cared who walked with her around school.

Muffin met her at the door, whining, and Denne wanted to whine, too, as soon as she heard the voices in the kitchen. She stood for a minute in the hallway, listening and soothing the cocker spaniel. Aunt Edith's strident voice floated out to her.

"You always were just as pretty as a picture, Alicia. When you were only a baby, I said, 'Now, Margaret, this one is going to break all the boys' hearts, you just watch and see!' and, sure enough, you are a real heartbreaker. You just remind me so much of myself when I was your age. . . ."

Margaret's aunt had arrived for her annual surprise visit. Ever since Denne could remember at some point every year Aunt Edith had suddenly appeared at their door. She had been just the same all these years, reliving her past triumphs as the belle of Carroll County and expecting Alicia and Denne to be just as popular as she had been, so she could experience it all again vicariously.

Briefly, Denne wondered if she dared try to sneak upstairs without being noticed. She decided that she wouldn't be able to, and putting her books on the hall table, she went into the kitchen with Muffin still whining at her heels. Aunt Edith wasn't one of Muffin's favorites, either.

Edith stood and enveloped Denne in her arms, almost smothering her against her portly front.

"Well, there you are, Denne. I've just been asking about you. You must sit right down and tell me all about your boyfriends!"

Denne sat beside her distinctly bored-looking sister, across the kitchen table from Edith. Her mother was moving around the kitchen, deep in dinner preparations.

"This is great; I have you side by side to compare," Aunt Edith stated, settling more comfortably into her chair, eager to get down to specifics. "Margaret, you have two very different daughters; I'll venture to say that people wouldn't even guess that they're sisters. Look at them, will you?" she demanded, as if Margaret had never noticed the differences between the girls. "I'd say you girls are opposites in just about every way; 'Licia, you're so fair as opposed to your dark features, Denne, and so well-rounded. Denne, dear, you are going to have to gain some weight and try to get a little bit of shape to your figure." Aunt Edith paused to take a sip from her ever-present cup of tea. Then she resumed. "Alicia has been telling me all about Michael, and now I want to hear about your Tom or Johnny or whoever you're all excited about these days. Or . . ." she paused to pick a piece of lint off the immaculate expanse of her navy blue bosom, "Maybe both of them. After all, you're way too young to tie yourself down to just one boy. At this stage you should be playing the field."

Nervously, Denne twisted one of her curls, wishing with all her might that she could flee. She looked at Alicia for help; if only she would say something, anything, to give Denne time to think of an answer that would satisfy the older woman. Alicia's face wore a mask of boredom; her eyes were glazed and far away. Denne turned to her mother, but Margaret had disappeared into the pantry.

"Well, Aunt Edith, really . . . there's nobody special just now," she stammered.

"Well, that's fine, just fine. You need to be going out with all kinds of different boys. Tell me, where do you all go on dates nowadays? I don't suppose you have any taffy pulls or hayrides. Do you just go to the movies or what?"

Denne was desperate; at the risk of starting an unending monologue, she asked, "What is a taffy pull, Aunt Edith? Did you go to lots of them when you were a girl?"

It worked. Edith started with a definition of taffy pull and proceeded through a detailed account of every such occasion she had ever attended, and named, described, and gave the family background of every boy who had ever escorted her to a taffy pull. By the time she had finished, Alicia was asleep with her eyes open, Denne had conjugated all her new French verbs in her head, Muffin was asleep with her eyes closed, and Margaret had finished dinner and was setting the table. Denne got up to help, but her escape wasn't complete. She had not outwitted Aunt Edith. As she went to the silverware drawer in the buffet in the adjoining dining room Aunt Edith called after her.

"You must try to be more like your sister, Denne. She is a cheerleader and she'll more than likely be homecoming queen, and she goes to every party in town, I'll bet. You must try to be more outgoing and get into more activities. If you'd try you could overcome your boyish figure and haircut. Why don't you let your hair grow long like Alicia's and maybe get a padded bra? You just have to learn to make the most of yourself, and even though you'll never compete with your sister, you can find a boyfriend if you really try!"

Denne gritted her teeth and wondered how long Aunt Edith planned to stay. With a sinking feeling she remembered that the lady usually stayed at least a week. Denne estimated that approximately two hours of that week had passed.

By Friday afternoon Denne was actually looking forward to Jan's visit. Maybe Aunt Edith would leave her alone if she were busy with a guest; all week she had been the center of Aunt Edith's attention. Alicia, of course, had been out with Michael a good deal of the time, and, since Denne was the one that her aunt felt really needed help, anyway, she poured out advice and examples of her own success for Denne to profit from in a never-ending stream. Denne had spent more time closeted in her room, supposedly studying, this week than in all the time school had been open put together. Thursday night Aunt Edith had remarked, "Well, I'll declare, you study more than any child I ever saw. You're taking it all way too seriously, honey. You need to be learning how to use makeup and shopping for some brighter, more feminine clothes!" So, it was with the sense of someone clutching at her last hope that Denne brought Jan into the house after school on Friday.

She felt a combination of relief and frustration to learn that her tormentor was at the beauty shop. "Wouldn't you know it," she said to Jan, "the one time I have some excuse to ignore her, she isn't even here!"

Margaret came up to Denne's room while the girls were changing out of their school clothes into jeans. She welcomed Jan, and then said, "Jan, I hope you won't think I'm rude if I don't cook dinner for you, but Denne's father and I are planning to take my aunt out to eat. You girls are welcome to join us."

The thought made Denne nauseous. "Thanks, Mom, but we won't have time; we're going to the early show. Why don't you and Dad just drop us off at the McDonald's around the corner from the theater?"

Margaret agreed and left to dress for the evening.

Jan was ready to go almost before Denne had hung up her school clothes; she sat turned sideways in Denne's desk chair, sizing up the room, going from the old-fashioned dresser Denne had refinished to the curlicued iron bedstead. "Is Alicia's room a lot like yours?" she asked.

Alicia's room was the farthest thing from Denne's mind; she paused a moment to try to catch Jan's train of thought.

"No, not really. She and Mom just decorated her room this summer. Would you like to see it?"

Jan nodded enthusiastically, her eyes shining.

Denne finished dressing, and on the way down the hall stopped in front of Alicia's door. "Well, there it is; you can decide for yourself how much it's like mine."

Jan, however, had forgotten Denne's room existed. "Oh, this is so cute," she gushed, her eyes busy taking in every detail. "All these ruffles and flowers look just like Alicia, don't they? I always think she has the best taste in clothes; I check every day at school to see what she's wearing."

Suddenly Denne felt an old familiar disappointment. She turned to Jan and gave her a long look, but all she said was, "We'd better go; my parents are probably waiting."

During dinner and before the movie Denne managed to keep the conversation on school and afterward, as she and Jan waited for her parents to pick them up, they talked about Robert Redford. On the ride home, of course, Aunt Edith did the talking; however, after she and Denne's parents had gone to the den to watch T.V. Denne was desperately wondering how she could entertain Jan another minute. Finally she suggested that they make a pizza, and she left Jan stirring the dough and went to put some records on the small phonograph on the sun porch.

When she came back in to help spread the dough

in the pan, Jan asked, "What time does Alicia usually get home from her dates?"

Mentally, Denne sighed. "Her curfew on weekends is midnight, and she usually gets home about two minutes after."

They had just closed the oven door on the pizza and Denne was putting out the Scrabble board on the kitchen table with Jan's lukewarm help when they heard the front door close.

Jan brightened. "Maybe that's Alicia now," she said.

"Can't be; it's way too early for her," Denne answered.

It was Alicia, though. She came directly to the kitchen and took a Coke from the refrigerator.

Denne tried to keep her voice calm. "What's wrong, 'Licia? Did you have a fight with Michael?"

"Um . . . maybe . . . I mean, sort of," Alicia answered vaguely, searching through a drawer for the bottle opener.

Denne introduced her sister to Jan, who was obviously thrilled.

"Alicia, do you want to play Scrabble?" she asked excitedly, as if that were her favorite game of all time.

"No, but I'll eat some of your pizza," she replied, and sat down across from Jan to sip her Coke.

There was a small silence, then Jan said, "I love that top, Alicia. It exactly matches your eyes."

"Thanks," Alicia answered briefly. She gave Jan a small smile, though, and that gave her courage to go on.

"Everybody's so excited about Demoiselles," she said. "I think every girl in school would join if she got an invitation. By the way, Alicia, when are the invitations going to be sent out?"

"I'm not sure; I think that it'll be next week, but it may be the week after next." Alicia watched Denne putting the Scrabble game back into the box. "Kathy Nolan is secretary and it'll depend on when she gets the invitations from the printer."

Jan prattled on, gradually drawing Alicia into a spirited discussion of the social club's planned projects for the year and of the cheerleaders' recent reorganization. By the time the pizza was ready to eat, Alicia was giving Jan advice about clothes and boys and Denne was munching in silence.

Alicia finished her second slice of pizza and brushed the crumbs into her napkin.

"Well, I wouldn't want to interfere in your kitchen work, so I'll go on to bed and let you girls clean up," she teased, putting the pan into the sink and running water in it as her contribution. She paused in the doorway. "It's been fun talking with you, Jan," she said. "See you." She gave Denne a little wave. " 'Night, Den."

Jan was humming as they put the kitchen back in order and went up to Denne's room. She didn't seem to notice that Denne was hardly talking at all.

"Alicia is really nice," she mumbled, pulling her sleep-shirt over her head.

"Yeah," Denne answered briefly. "Listen, Jan, would you mind terribly if we just go to bed now? I am really tired all of a sudden."

"That's O.K. with me," Jan replied, "I feel as if I've done a lot today."

Denne pulled the sheet over them and switched out the lamp beside the bed. Jan's voice came softly from beside her. "You know, Denne," she said dreamily, snuggling into her pillow, "I've wanted to be a member of Demoiselles ever since I was in junior high. In fact, almost as long as I can remember." She yawned once, and almost instantly was asleep.

Denne lay awake for a long time, trying not to move and disturb Jan. She certainly didn't want to have to talk to her anymore, she thought. If only there were some way to get her out of the room and back to her own house! Denne sighed. I'll have to put up with her until tomorrow morning, she decided, but maybe I can say I have a contagious disease and get Mom to take her home when she takes Aunt Edith to the airport at 6:30. However and whenever Jan went home, Denne was determined that it would be long before the customary noon on Saturday.

She turned onto her side very carefully and stared out at the shadows the tree limbs were making against the pale moonlight. The feeling of disappointment that had come as soon as she realized why Jan was there came back more strongly than ever. She's worse than Aunt Edith, she thought bitterly. At least Aunt Edith is honest about preferring Alicia.

Everybody prefers Alicia, she thought, tears coming suddenly to her eyes; Michael popped into her mind as the most important of those everybodys. She blinked back the tears and forced herself to concentrate on the shadows. I have to do something, she thought. If I don't change the way things are, I'm going to be so far back in Alicia's shadow that no one will see me at all.

11

Monday morning Denne reached the kitchen just as Margaret was plugging in the coffeepot. "My goodness, Denne, whatever are you doing up so early? And you're all dressed and ready to go."

"I have a meeting before school; the All-School Board, remember?" Denne answered. "And I wanted to be able to walk slowly and enjoy the morning. Pretty soon the leaves will be gone and it'll be too cold to really enjoy walking."

"I can understand that. Just take a few minutes to eat something before you go, though, O.K.?" Margaret turned to give Denne a loving smile. "You know Aunt Edith wants you to get some meat on your bones, so you need to eat!" she teased.

Denne chuckled. "Dear Aunt Edith! I'll bet you're up early, Mom, just to enjoy the quiet in your own kitchen."

"There could be some truth in that," Margaret smiled. "I must admit that one of my fondest dreams for the day is to read the paper and drink my coffee in peace."

Denne had toast, juice and a scrambled egg, then gathered her books and came back through the kitchen to tell her mother good-bye. "Remember I have to tutor after school today, so I'll be late," she reminded Margaret.

Denne did indeed walk very slowly toward school. The big arching trees along Evans Road were fascinating to her in any season, but they were especially wonderful in the fall. The early sun seemed to draw its yellow glow from the leaves and the color filled the morning air. Denne picked up a perfect leaf, one of the largest she'd seen from an elm, and twirled its stem in her fingers as she walked.

Her mind was twirling, too, full of the thoughts and resolves that had come to her these past two days. I'm not going to be another Jan, she vowed again, I'm not going to try to be like Alicia or do the things she does. I intend to be my own person; I can excel in other things besides my grades; I'll be accepted in my own way—I'll just join different activities and do different things from the ones she's involved in. I'll show Aunt Edith and everybody else that I don't have to be another Alicia.

Her thoughts raced ahead to the All-School Board meeting. That's something Alicia isn't in, she thought. It's a good way to learn about school policies and to meet some more people, and it has nothing whatsoever to do with my sister!

Denne went up the steps to the front entrance of the school thinking that surely if she tried hard enough she could come completely out of Alicia's shadow and become permanently the Denne she had been for a couple of months this summer.

Several people were already in Mr. Monro's conference room when Denne arrived. As she slid into one of the chairs at the long table, she felt important and responsible, ready to help run the school. The other members of the board gathered rapidly, and Mr. Monro began the meeting at the scheduled 7:30 starting time. First, he had everyone tell his name and position in the school. There were two or three teachers whom Denne didn't know, and several students who were new to her. This will be perfect, she thought, I'll get to know quite a few people this way, and maybe even get into some more activities through them.

Mr. Monro made a few preliminary announcements and then announced the first item on the agenda. "We need to evaluate the process we have been using for the student council elections," he said. "Some people have suggested that we need a longer campaign period and an assembly earlier in that time to introduce the candidates, instead of having them appear before the entire student body for the first time on the day of the election. It is my feeling that we should set up a committee to gather some opinions about this from throughout the school and to make some recommendations based on those findings." He paused and looked around the table. "Denne," he said, and Denne jumped, surprised to hear her name. "Denne, would you please serve as the chairperson of that committee? I know that you were a recent candidate for a position on the student council, and your experience might be helpful in looking into this."

"I . . . all right, Mr. Monro, I'll do my best," she

replied. She felt nervous about being singled out and put to work so soon, but she also felt pleased that Mr. Monro had remembered who she was as well as the fact that she had run for student council. As he went on to suggest other committee members to work with her she was thinking, My new resolution is already working—I'm becoming a person in my own right already.

Finally all the members of her committee had been chosen, and Mr. Monro turned back to her. "Now, Denne, as chairperson, you will be responsible for setting up the meetings of your committee, making individual assignments, and making sure that everything is done." He gave her a smile. "If you need any help, just let me know."

"Thank you, Mr. Monro, I will," she replied, feeling very capable.

Mr. Monro moved on to the other item of business for today's meeting. "You may not be aware of this, but it is just under a month until our scheduled homecoming football game and dance. There are a great many preparations to be made, of course, for these important events. We must form committees today and get right to work if we are to complete the plans on time. Since this will be something which will require a great deal of your time, I would like for each of you to work on a committee that you would especially enjoy. I'm going to pass around this sheet which lists all the committees, and I'd like for you to look them over carefully and sign up for the one of your choice. While we are doing that, Mrs. Kirby will serve us some doughnuts and coffee or hot chocolate. Please just be sure that you leave the sign-up sheets with me before you go. Thank you so much for coming; I know that this is going to be one of the most efficient, hardworking All-School Boards that we've had in a number of years," he concluded with a smile.

Mrs. Kirby placed boxes of doughnuts and stacks of napkins in the middle of the long table, and one by one, everyone got up to help himself to a cup of coffee or hot chocolate. A boy sitting next to Denne, who had been introduced as Tim Braden, offered to get her some hot chocolate, so she took one of the homecoming committee sheets and began to think about her choices. A list was printed across the top of the page, then each committee title was reprinted below with spaces for at least four names under each one: SELECTION OF QUEEN AND ATTENDANTS; CORONATION ARRANGEMENTS; DANCE THEME AND DECORATIONS; DANCE REFRESHMENTS; CLEANUP AFTER THE DANCE. Mr. Sloane, the art teacher, was sitting across from her reading a copy of the same list. "Well, there's one committee on this sheet that we can just eliminate and save ourselves a lot of time and trouble," he announced to the group in general.

Mr. Monro asked, "Which one is that?"

"Why, this committee to select the queen for homecoming," he answered. "Everyone in school knows that Alicia Drake is going to be elected; nobody else can even come close."

Everyone chuckled, and Mr. Monro replied, "I have no doubt that you are absolutely right, Mr. Sloane. However, we do need someone to set up the balloting, to count the votes and to announce the results. After all, we must be fair to Alicia's competition, if she has any."

Mr. Sloane shook his head. "She doesn't have any. That girl has the most perfect face. I always think she looks like a painting."

Mrs. Owens, the home economics teacher, chimed in. "She *is* a beautiful girl, and she dresses well. When she was in my class last year I told her that it was amazing how she could always be so well-groomed and still be so active in so many different areas. I think Alicia just has a tremendous amount of energy: she's a member of almost every club in school."

"Yet she keeps her grades up pretty well, too," Mr. Monro said. "She has all B's and C's every time we do an eligibility check for her; her gradepoint average won't keep her out of the running."

Mrs. Owens said, half-teasingly, "You know, we might as well plan the theme and the colors around her."

The girl sitting next to Mrs. Owens, Carrie Green, took that very seriously. "That's a great idea! Let's make the background at the coronation and behind the throne at the dance a dark color so it'll highlight her hair. We could pick other colors that would go with it for the other decorations."

Denne wanted to get up and leave the room. Her new resolutions for becoming a real person all on her own faded away and she felt invisible once more; even in her important new activity she was in Alicia's shadow again, and Alicia wasn't even there. She felt trapped. I should just go back to being my old studious reclusive self, she thought. What's the point of trying to get into new activities if everything is going to be Alicia, Alicia, just the way it always has been?

Her thoughts came back to the conversation just

in time to hear Mr. Monro saying ". . . don't be too hasty; the selection hasn't been made yet." He smiled. "However, if you want to be prepared, you might ask Denne here what her sister's favorite colors are."

Mrs. Owens and Carrie Green leaned across the table toward Denne with identical looks of astonishment on their faces. "You're Alicia's sister?" they chorused.

"Yes," Denne replied shortly, and reached for the sheet for the committee assignments. Under DANCE REFRESHMENTS she scrawled her name, then leaving the sheet lying on the table, she pushed back her chair. "I really have to go now," she said to no one in particular as she left the room.

12

Denne walked down the hallway blindly, instinctively going in the direction of her locker. This is the way it always will be, she thought. I'll be introduced as Alicia Drake's sister for the rest of my life.

She stood in front of her locker too preoccupied to choose the books she needed for her morning classes. The halls were filling up with students now that it was almost time for homeroom, but she didn't see anyone. She just felt numb, trapped in a feeling of hopelessness about herself and this school year. Sharon's voice at her elbow startled her into attention.

"Hi, Denne! How are things with you? Is Aunt Edith still here? Did you have a good time with Jan? In other words, how was your weekend and are you ready for yet another Monday morning at dear old Clinton High?"

Sharon's monologue drew a weak smile from Denne. "I guess I'm O.K., Sharon. It's just that . . . well, it's the same old thing all the time. Everywhere I go everyone is talking about Alicia and all the things she does; compared to her I'm always a nobody and I am just sick of it." Her frustration was so strong that the words poured out. For once Denne didn't need her usual private setting and roundabout preliminaries to tell Sharon about her personal feelings; this time she couldn't stop them. "Sharon, I wish I could go to another school, a school where no one had ever heard of my sister!" Denne's slender fingers gripped the handle on her locker door so hard it was cutting into them. "And now I am on a committee for the homecoming dance, so I'll have to go to it—without a date, no doubt—and there she'll be, reigning over the entire school! I just can't take it anymore!" she wailed.

Sharon was her usual comforting, capable self. "Denne, please don't be so upset. Don't panic; let's take one thing at a time. Now tell me what's happened."

Denne gave her a brief description of the meeting she'd just left, ending with "Why in the world did I ever get on that board in the first place? If I weren't on it I wouldn't be on a committee, and I wouldn't have to go to the dance. I could just stay home!" She looked into Sharon's blue eyes with a desperate plea, as if Sharon could get her out of her obligations and let her stay home.

Sharon was very quiet, and when Denne became aware of that, she could see that the wheels were turning fast under the frizzy red hair. "We'll deal with the date-for-the-dance problem first," she announced. "Once you know you have a date for it you are going to feel *much* better. When that is settled for sure, we'll go on to the next problem. Now listen to me and don't interrupt," Sharon ordered, looking at Denne intensely. "I've already mentioned to Joe the possibility of getting you and Reece together, and he really liked the idea. So I'll get busy on that today and see if Reece can take you to the dance. The four of us will go together, and we can all help you with your committee stuff, whatever you have to do." The warning bell shrilled down the hallway. Sharon gave Denne a quick hug and ran for her homeroom class.

Denne sat through homeroom like a zombie, and English started out the same way. Sharon's idea had given her hope, although she hated to admit it. The thought of a blind date was certainly unappealing, but so was the thought of appearing alone to watch Alicia's triumph. Maybe all is not lost, after all, she thought; maybe I shouldn't give up all my new resolutions the minute I have one little setback. The thought comforted her, and she turned her attention to Mrs. Ulrich at last.

". . . It will be approximately two weeks until we hold the tryouts for *As You Like It.* I hope that many of you in this class will participate, and if you don't get parts, I hope you will work backstage. The experience will greatly enhance your understanding of Shakespeare; I know you will find it tremendously rewarding."

I think I will try out, Denne thought. It would be such a release for my emotions to be in a play again, and it would give me a little confidence in myself, the way it did last summer. Then a picture of herself and Alicia on the stage, trying out, floated into her mind.

Well, she thought, maybe she'll be too busy. If she doesn't try out, I am definitely going to! she promised herself.

The possibility of being in the play or at least working on it backstage kept popping up in Denne's mind off and on all day. At times she thought she would try out even if Alicia did, and take a smaller part; at other times she decided to try for the part of Rosalind if Alicia didn't.

After dinner that evening, Denne went to her room and attempted to study, but she kept thinking of all the things that had happened that day and the idea of trying out for the play came back into her head. It was more appealing than ever; she just didn't want to get too excited about it if it were destined to go the way of her other plans. Finally she put down her pen and wandered down the hall to Alicia's door.

Alicia was sprawled across the bed on her stomach, rapidly copying information from one spiral notebook into another.

"Hi, Alicia. Are you too busy to talk a little? I'm too restless to study," Denne said.

Alicia happily threw down her pen. "I am so sick of trying to make sense out of chemistry that I would be glad if you'd sit here and talk the rest of the night and give me an excuse to ignore it!" she replied.

Denne settled into the overstuffed armchair and, kicking off her shoes, she curled her feet up under her. "Well, I've been trying to read *As You Like It* for English tomorrow, but I can't concentrate, either. Mrs. Ulrich was talking about the junior-senior play again today, and I keep thinking about how much fun it would be to try out." Denne twisted one of her curls and looked into her sister's big blue eyes.

"I can't decide whether I have time to do it or not," she said, making her voice as casual as possible.

"Well, I know *I* don't have time to do it," Alicia declared. "If they'd wait until a little bit later in the school year to give the play I might be able to, but with cheerleading and getting ready for homecoming and everything, I'm going to do well to keep my grades and my eligibility." Worriedly, Alicia chewed on the end of her pen. "I'm getting scared about my chemistry grades; if Brad Fitzgerald didn't let me copy his notes, I don't know what I'd do. I can't understand the lectures enough to take decent ones of my own."

"What grades are you making in there?" Denne asked. "You'll be eligible for homecoming queen, won't you?"

Alicia's face creased into an uncharacteristic frown. "I'd better be," she said in a determined voice. "I have a C right now, and if I can make a C on the quiz next week I'll be O.K."

"Oh, Alicia, you'll make it, I know you will. There'd probably be a riot if you weren't queen; everyone is already saying that you will be," Denne tried to reassure her.

Alicia seemed to have drifted off into her thoughts, but the last part of Denne's statement penetrated the fog and she brightened. "Really? Oh, that's good," she smiled. The faraway look stayed in her eyes, though. Suddenly she blurted, "If Brad would only ask me to the Homecoming dance, the whole thing would just be perfect. He is so good-looking and such a good captain of the team. It would be like a movie or something if he could crown me at the game and then escort me to the dance that night." She sighed wistfully at the picture in her mind.

Denne gasped, but Alicia was lost in her dream world and she didn't notice.

"He is the handsomest boy at school and it would be so neat, like a play or something, if we could be together for all of the homecoming celebrations," she mused.

Denne found her tongue. "Sort of costar throughout the movie, you mean?" she asked sarcastically.

Alicia, oblivious to the tone of Denne's question, nodded. "Yeah, something like that."

"But what about Michael?" Denne said softly, her voice shaking a little. "Are you just planning to dump him?"

Alicia raised her eyes to Denne's. "Listen, Den," she said quickly, "don't breathe a word of this to a soul, O.K.? I really didn't mean to tell my pipedream out loud. Promise not to tell?"

Denne nodded.

"Cross your heart and hope to die?" Alicia asked anxiously, just as they had done since they were little girls.

Denne crossed her heart.

"Don't worry, I'm not dumping Michael," Alicia said soothingly. "This is just a fantasy that'll never come true. Even if it did, I'd still want to date Michael, too." Alicia rolled over and sat up, leaning back against the fluffy pillows with the ruffled shams. "Really, though, it would probably be good for our relationship to date other people sometimes," she stated, her face serious.

Suddenly Denne sat up straight, her feet on the floor, her hands gripping the big arms of the chair.

"You're moving up again, aren't you, Alicia? You're going from football player to football captain just the way you went from basketball player to football player when you dropped poor Bob for Michael!" she accused.

Alicia smiled, not a trace of guilt in her eyes. "Well, you want me to be ambitious, don't you? You surely don't want your sister to stagnate and never move up in the world," she said teasingly.

"Well, I . . . I just don't want you to hurt Michael the way you did Bob," Denne stammered. "He's too nice a person. And what about Kathy Nolan? How is she going to feel when you steal her boyfriend?"

Alicia's long red nails clicked down the spiral spine of the notebook Brad had loaned her. "I think they're having some trouble," she said. "I doubt they'll be going steady much longer." Alicia sat up straighter and arranged her books in front of her. "Don't take any of this seriously, Denne," she said in her most sincere way. "Brad doesn't think of me as someone to date, he's just my buddy in Chemistry I. I never see him anywhere without Kathy." She shook her long hair back over her shoulders and looked down at the notebooks.

Denne stood up, knowing she'd been dismissed. "Well, I'll go and let you get to work. We certainly don't want your grades to keep you from being queen and ruin the movie."

Alicia agreed. "Right. Back to the sodium mines as we say in the world of chemistry!"

Denne went back to her room with a fury of emotions churning inside her. It's so unfair! she thought, over and over again. Alicia always has, always does, and always will get every single thing that she wants. She wanted Michael and she got him, and now, no matter how much she says she won't, she'll get Brad.

Automatically, Denne sat down at her desk and stared unseeingly at her books while her mind continued to go in circles on the subject of her sister. She's not only going to get Brad just because he has struck her fancy, but she is going to manage to keep Michael, too. I don't have the faintest idea of how she is going to do it, but I know she can. She'll have both of them wrapped around her little finger.

Denne pushed her books away disgustedly and walked restlessly over to the window, staring out at the big tree she loved. How is it that my sister can be the most beautiful girl in school and date the two most popular boys and I can't even go to a stupid All-School Board meeting and make an impression as anything but her sister? I can't make a new friend on my own who isn't just interested in talking to Alicia, I can't measure up to Alicia in our relative's eyes, I can't even get elected to the student council, much less homecoming queen!

Disgusted, Denne turned from the window and gathered up her robe and slippers, preparing to go take her shower. Her thoughts moved to Michael.

If she goes out with Brad, it'll really hurt him, she thought. He'll be hurt and upset and he'll probably start doing badly in French again. Who knows, he might even lose his scholarship.

She went down the hall to the bathroom, turned on the water and adjusted the temperature, then she stepped in. The full force of the water hit her shoulders at the same time a new thought struck her mind. He'll be hurt, and he'll need to talk about it, she thought. And we're becoming friends—I talk to him about my problems, maybe he'll talk to me about his! Maybe he'll talk it all over with me and we'll become really close friends!

That thought stayed with Denne all the way into bed. We may become very close, she repeated, as she dropped off to sleep.

13

Denne waited for Michael to come to Thursday afternoon's tutoring session with a feeling she hadn't had since the very first time they had met in this room. Ever since her talk with Alicia on Monday night Michael had been in the back of her mind almost constantly and she had wondered over and over again whether he would ever think of her as someone to date. Now that he was going to appear at any minute, all the old feelings of panic and excitement were welling up in Denne again. She arranged their chairs in the usual way then she paced around the room, flipped unseeingly through the big world atlas on its stand, and ended up standing in front of the windows, staring out at the leaf-strewn campus.

When the door opened, Denne turned. Michael's tall form seemed to fill the doorway, and Denne thought again how good-looking he was. He was wearing faded jeans with a blue and white striped Western shirt open at the neck. His tan stood out against the collar and the sleeves that were rolled halfway up his muscular arms. Denne couldn't take her eyes off him and she couldn't think of a thing to say.

Here I am back at square one, she thought. We have actually become friends these past few weeks, but if I start being so self-conscious again I'll ruin that. And if I don't stop thinking about how good he looks and how much I wish I could reach out and touch him I will never be able to get through this hour!

Michael walked over to stand beside her. His closeness made Denne's heart pound furiously. She forced her eyes away from him and fastened them on the large maple trees that lined the street in front of the school.

"You seem to be off somewhere in a world of your own," he said, in a teasing voice. "What are you so interested in out there?"

Frantically Denne tried to think of an answer. "Oh, I was just looking at the leaves—I love the colors."

"But what were you thinking about?" he persisted. "You were a million miles away when I came in."

Denne obviously couldn't admit she'd been thinking about him, so she searched her mind for a topic, any topic, that would sound absorbing enough to be believable. Finally she said, "I'm trying to decide whether or not to try out for the junior-senior play. Mrs. Ulrich says casting will begin in a few days."

"Have you ever been in a play?" Michael's tone showed that he was so immediately involved in her interests that Denne forgot about being self-conscious.

"This summer at camp I had the lead in *Can-Can,*" she answered.

"Did you like doing it?" he asked.

She nodded. "Very much. It was the most exciting thing I've ever done. I loved the challenge and I especially loved the applause," she smiled.

Even as she spoke, Denne couldn't believe that once again she was talking to Michael about her personal feelings.

"Well, then, it's settled," he announced. "You are going to try out. I don't understand why you even had any doubts about it."

He was so genuinely interested that Denne blurted, "Oh, it's different here from the way it was at camp." Then she stopped. She was aching to tell him how frustrated she had been these last few days trying to make a place for herself as an individual and how she was beginning to be afraid to try for fear she'd just have to face another defeat. She didn't want him to think that she was always feeling sorry for herself; that session after she had lost the student council election had been enough to give him the impression that she was a big crybaby.

She bit her lip and forced a light tone into her voice. "The competition around here is a whole lot stiffer," she said. "I'd hate to be rejected after my recent triumph."

Michael looked squarely into her eyes. "You don't have to worry about the competition," he said. "You just go right into those tryouts and read for the leading role, do you hear me?" He frowned with mock sternness.

Denne laughed. "I hear you! Your word is my

command." She turned away from the window. "We'd better get busy or this whole hour will go by and you'll get out of all your work," she told him. "I don't intend to let you out of here today until I find out whether you've learned the answer to the question, *'Dis donc, où est la bibliothèque?'* "

Michael laughed as they slid into their chairs. "I've answered that one wrong so many times I doubt I'll ever get it right," he said.

As usual, Muffin met Denne at the door. She put her books on the table and knelt down to pat her head. Muffin rolled over contentedly to have her tummy scratched.

"Denne? Is that you?" Margaret called from the kitchen.

"Yes, Mom. Are you making cookies? I'm starved!" Denne replied, giving Muffin one last tickle and heading in the direction of the chocolate-chip aroma.

She found Margaret sliding the first dozen from the thin baking sheet to the cooling rack. "How was your day, dear?" she asked. "Anything world-shaking happen?"

"If you mean did Mr. Monro tell me he could get me a full scholarship to Yale or was I commissioned to paint a masterpiece to decorate the main lobby of First National Bank, the answer is no. However," she mumbled, her mouth full of cookie, "I did have a very good tutoring session with Michael." It sent a little thrill through Denne to casually say his name like that.

Her mother didn't seem to notice anything unusual about it. "That's great, Den. It'll be good if you can help him get that scholarship; that was all he talked about the other night when he was here waiting for Alicia."

Denne went to the refrigerator and poured herself a glass of milk as Margaret began dropping the next batch of cookies onto the baking sheet.

"Alicia just called," she said with a smile. "She found out a few minutes ago that she was elected homecoming queen!"

Denne looked at her mother over the rim of her glass. "Well, I guess she got her C in chemistry, then. That's good—she was going to be really disappointed if she weren't elected."

"Yes, I think it's nice—it's an honor," Margaret replied. "I suppose there'll be a formal announcement of some kind at school tomorrow." She slid the new tray of cookies into the oven, then turned to Denne.

"Oh, I almost forgot," she said. "The mail's there on the counter. Something's in it for you."

Denne picked up the letters and magazines and carried them to the table. She flipped through them quickly and as soon as she came to the small white envelope addressed in perfectly round letters she knew what it was.

"Oh, this is my invitation to join Demoiselles," she said. "I figured I'd be getting one; after all, how could they leave out Alicia's sister?"

"Now, Denne, you aren't being fair. I'm sure you are being invited for yourself and what you can contribute to the club," her mother replied firmly.

"Oh, Mom, you're such a dreamer," Denne said a trifle bitterly. "There's no way I'm popular enough on my own to be invited to join the Clinton High Chapter of the Red Cross, much less a social club. Especially not the very *best* social club!"

"Well, if you are too stubborn to see your own attractions, I'm not going to argue with you. Whatever the reason you've been asked, I think it would be very good for you to join. You'd make some new friends and all the club's activities would give you lots of new things to do." Margaret came to sit across from Denne at the round table in the middle of the kitchen. She took a cookie and bit into it absentmindedly. "You need some social life, Denne, and this just might give it to you," she observed.

For a minute Denne munched cookies and thought about what her mother had just said. It was very true that Demoiselles were kept busy almost constantly with service activities and events to raise money to finance them. They also had several big parties during the school year and Denne knew that almost all of the interesting boys in school would come to them. It might be possible for her to learn how to relate to boys if she attended enough social occasions like those. She might even meet someone who would be as attractive to her as Michael was.

She tried to imagine what it would be like and as soon as the images formed in her mind she began shaking her head.

"It would never work, Mom, don't you see?" She looked into Margaret's blue eyes, now dark with concern. "From the very first minute I would be introduced as Alicia's sister, and everyone would be gathered around saying '*You* are Alicia Drake's sister? I can't believe it, you aren't a thing like her!' I am so sick of that, Mom, I just can't stand it any more." Denne took a big gulp of milk to try to cover the fact that tears of frustration were beginning to form in her eyes. "I really don't know how to do it, but somehow I have to find some things to do on my own that have nothing to do with Alicia," she said, her voice a little unsteady.

Margaret looked at her keenly and gave her hand a pat. Then she got up to take the cookies out of the oven.

"You may be right, Denne," she said. "It's just that I don't see what harm it could do to let Alicia help you meet some people and sort of get you started with the kids in the Upper-Class Building. After all, she has been there a year already."

Denne stood up quickly and took her glass to the sink to rinse it out. "Well, it would be good if things could be that way, but it won't work. I just don't want to always be hanging around in Alicia's shadow failing people who are expecting me to be a carbon copy of her." Denne walked to the door and stopped. She turned to look directly at her mother. "I can't join Demoiselles, Mom. More and more I'm realizing that I have to learn to be an individual all my own."

Margaret nodded. "All right. You can do that, Denne, if it's what you want. Just let me know if I can help."

"I will, Mom, thanks," Denne answered. She called back over her shoulder, "I just hope Jan got one of these invitations. There's no way I can take another weekend with her while she tries to get an explanation out of Alicia!" Margaret's laugh followed her up the stairs.

As Denne passed the phone in the upstairs hallway, it rang. Sharon's voice was elated. "It's all set, Den. Reece will be your escort for the homecoming festivities!"

Denne was numb. "Uh, oh, fine. Thanks, Sharon."

"You don't seem too terribly thrilled. What's wrong? You'll like him, Denne, I really think you will, and even if you don't, we'll have a good time. You can just talk to me and ignore him if you hate him."

Denne laughed. "All right, I will. I really do appreciate this, Sharon."

"I've got to go, Joe's waiting. I just wanted to let you know."

"O.K., thanks. See you tomorrow."

Denne was suddenly overcome by a terrible depression. She went into her rocm and slumped on the bed. She kicked off her shoes and curled her feet under her, plumped two pillows behind her back and settled down to think. The thought of a blind date scared her to death. Oh, why, *why* did I let myself in for this? she moaned. What if this Reece turns out to be a head shorter than I am or something equally awful? Her stomach tightened and she chewed her thumbnail.

Surely, he must have something wrong with him or he wouldn't have to depend on his friends to get him blind dates. Oh, being seen at homecoming with him will be worse than not going at all!

She snatched a patchwork pillow and hugged it to her. I should have told Sharon to forget it, she thought. I could have just slipped in to do my committee work and then come home again, but now I'll have to spend the entire evening embarrassing myself once again in front of the entire student body of Clinton High!

Denne sat up straight as an even more important objection came to her in a flash.

She didn't really want a date unless it was with Michael. I want to go to homecoming with Michael!

she thought, punching the pillow hard. I was secretly hoping Alicia would go with Brad and that Michael would ask me. Instead, I now have a date with someone I don't even know—if Michael asked me, I'd have to say no.

The irony of that made Denne laugh out loud. This is so smart; here I am lying around worrying about what to do if Michael should ask me to homecoming, and there is approximately one chance in a trillion that he would even think of doing such a thing! Come on, Denne, face reality and be glad you aren't going to the game and the dance alone. She gave herself a good shake and got up and changed into jeans and a sweat shirt. Bounding down the stairs, she found Muffin hanging around the door. "Come on, girl," she said, ruffling one silky ear, "let's go for a little run before dinnertime."

14

The Saturday of the game was clear and very crisp, the coldest day yet this fall. Denne dressed in her chocolate-colored corduroy jeans, an off-white wool sweater and the hooded rabbit-fur jacket she'd bought on sale at the end of last winter. It was dyed in stripes of white and dark brown, and when she looked at herself in the mirror, she was pleased. Her thick curls and her wide eyes matched the brown shades and the whites blended with her sweater. For once I look all pulled together, she thought, smiling at her reflection. If only I can *feel* pulled together after I see my date! she thought.

The doorbell rang as Denne was going down the stairs. She answered it to find a stocky boy who, much to her relief, was about three inches taller than her own 5′4″. His narrow gray eyes moved quickly from the hood of her jacket down her entire body to her brown boots, then they came back to rest appraisingly on her face.

"You must be Denne," he said. "I'm Reece."

"Hello, Reece," she replied. He really isn't bad looking at all, she decided, as she checked her purse for her keys.

"You ready? Joe and Sharon are waiting in the car."

Denne nodded. "Bye, Mom I'm gone," she called, and when she heard Margaret's good-bye she stepped outside and closed the door behind her.

Reece took her elbow to guide her to the car, starting to talk before they even got down the steps. "I'm really looking forward to seeing this game. Clinton has such a good reputation this year, and Webb City always has the best team in the conference, so it should be a real battle."

He opened the back door of Joe's parents' car for Denne, then almost slammed it on her foot before she could step in and get settled. I guess he really is in a hurry to get to the game, Denne thought.

Sharon turned around to sit sideways against the door so she could talk with Denne. Her face was glowing with pleasure at the success of her plans.

"You look great, Sharon," Denne said, as Reece was climbing into the other side of the backseat.

"Thanks, so do you," her friend smiled back. "I am so excited about this. I just know we're going to have a great day," she went on.

Reece interrupted. "We will if we get decent seats so we can see the game. Come on, Joe, let's get going."

They arrived at the stadium in plenty of time to sit near the fifty-yard line and as soon as they were settled the boys went to the concession stand for hot chocolate to help keep them warm. Sharon turned to Denne, her eyes glowing.

"Well, Denne, what do you think? Do you like Reece? I think he likes you."

"Sharon, how can you possibly say that? He doesn't even know I'm here. All he cares about is talking to Joe about football."

"Maybe he's just shy and is covering up his nervousness that way," Sharon said thoughtfully. She brightened. "I really think that's it," she said. "After the game he'll probably be a lot more interesting because there'll be other things to talk about."

Denne shrugged. "We'll see," she answered, her initial relief about Reece's appearance fading into total frustration over his behavior.

Reece continued to talk about football all during the first half, but as soon as the half-time ceremonies began Denne found that there was, indeed, something else that he was interested in. The queen's attendants were escorted onto the platform in the center of the field, and then Alicia came out on the arms of two players to meet Brad, who was waiting to crown her homecoming queen. She was dressed in Clinton's colors: a pale blue dress with a wide gold sash across one shoulder which bore the words, Clinton Homecoming Queen. Her long blonde hair was shining in the bright sunlight and the cold breeze didn't seem to disturb it at all.

Reece gave a low whistle. "Man, would you look at that!" he said, leaning across both girls to get Joe's attention as he had done on the average of every five minutes during the game. "She is a beauty! Joe, who is that gorgeous creature?"

Denne had a sudden urge to give his solid form a push and send him sprawling off his seat into the laps of the people below.

"That's Alicia Drake," Joe answered. "She's Denne's sister."

Reece shook his head as if he believed he hadn't heard correctly. Sharon repeated, "Alicia is Denne's sister. She's a senior this year."

Reece sat back in his seat and stared down at Denne. He looked from her to the smiling Alicia, who was allowing Brad to place the crown on her head. "*She* is your sister?" he asked, disbelief written all over his face.

Abruptly, Denne nodded, not trusting herself to speak.

"Boy, you sure don't look anything like her!" he declared, and he spent the remainder of half time staring at Queen Alicia.

When they arrived at Jamod's Steakhouse Denne entered with a sigh of relief. Then she realized that she didn't know why she should feel that way, she was still with Reece and no one in the restaurant was going to rescue her. At least, she thought, I'll manage not to sit between him and Joe, so maybe I'll be able to breathe.

They ordered, then Sharon and Denne went to the powder room. "Well, Sharon," Denne said, "another of your famous predictions has come true. If I am going to have a good time today at all, I'm going to have to talk exclusively to you."

"Denne, I am so sorry." Sharon's face crumpled with disappointment. "He is just the rudest person, and I don't know what to do about it."

"Oh, Sharon, it's not your fault. Face it, if I'd ever learned the first thing about being interesting to boys, I would be able to keep his attention. I knew I'd never know how to act on a date and I was right!"

"No, don't feel that way. You'd be a really fun date for the right boy. I've gotten you into this fiasco and now it's going to ruin your attitude about all boys forever!" she wailed.

Her distress touched Denne. "Oh, please Sharon," she said, going to put her arm around her friend, "please don't worry. I can stand him the rest of the day. You did the best you could—you had no way of knowing what he would be like." Sharon sank onto a chair, seeming about to cry. Denne rushed to reassure her. "At least I won't have to go to the dance without a date, and that's what I was dreading the most. And I'm on that committee, so I'll have to help with the refreshments and I won't be with him all that much this evening. Oh, please, Sharon," she pleaded. "Please don't cry."

Sharon blinked and swallowed hard. "O.K., but Denne, I promise never to put you in such a situation again."

"It's O.K., let's just do the best we can to get through all the rest of this," Denne replied, as they went back into the dining room. She wished she could slip out the back door and disappear.

All during dinner Denne concentrated on her food and on shutting out the sound of Reece's voice. Joe made several attempts to change the subject from a play-by-play rehash of the game, but Reece came back to it over and over again.

Finally Sharon couldn't take any more. "We'd better be going," she said. "My things are in the trunk of the car so I can dress at Denne's house, but you guys have to drive all the way out to Joe's to get ready. We can't be late to the dance because Denne's on the refreshment committee."

That got them moving and a few minutes later the boys left Sharon and Denne at Denne's front door. When they went into her room, Denne took off her coat, threw it on a chair, and collapsed onto the bed.

"I cannot leave this room, ever again," she declared. "I am totally exhausted, and if I hear that voice once more today, my ears will fall off."

"Man, did you see that interception?" Sharon rasped, in such a perfect imitation of Reece's voice that both girls dissolved into giggles.

Sharon recovered first, and fell into her usual habit of organizing things. "We only have two hours," she said, "because you need to be there early. Why don't you shower first so you can use your blow dryer while I shower and then I'll use it? I forgot to bring mine."

"All right," Denne said rapidly pulling off her boots and then her sweater and jeans. She grabbed her terrycloth robe and started for the door. "I'll let you organize my preparations for the evening, but never again will I let you arrange my dates!" Sharon threw a pillow at her just as she ducked out into the hallway.

When they arrived at the dance Denne felt the same kind of relief she had at the restaurant, but this time she had some justification for it. She turned to Reece and said, "I'll have to spend most of the evening helping serve refreshments, I'm afraid, Reece. I know that Joe and Sharon will take good care of you, though, and will introduce you to lots of people you can ask to dance."

Reece's eyes were scanning the sparse early

crowd. "Huh, oh, yeah, O.K.," he mumbled absentmindedly. "Sure, Denne, see you later."

Gratefully Denne headed for the long table set up at the side of the room to take her place behind the punch bowl.

A few minutes later people started coming in and before long the room was almost full. The tempo of the band's selections began to pick up, and so did traffic at Denne's station. She stayed very busy serving and going back and forth to the kitchen area for more punch and for Cokes, coffee and hot chocolate. When Sally Blair, the girl who was to take over for her finally showed up Denne told her to go ahead and dance. "I don't want to dance, really, Sally," Denne said. "I'd much rather just do this, O.K.?"

"Well, if you're sure, Denne. Thanks," Sally answered, rushing off to find her date again.

A few minutes later, Denne heard a now-familiar voice. "I'd like a Coke please," Reece said. Denne was getting it for him and trying to think of something pleasant to say when everyone turned to see Alicia, this time in a long clinging dress, still pale blue with the gold sash intact, coming into the room on Michael's arm. She was beaming from all the attention, and he was smiling down at her, just as he had done that very first time Denne had seen him. He looked so handsome in his black jacket that a lump caught in Denne's throat. Oh, how I would love to be with him . . . she thought, I'd feel so secure with my arm in his.

Reece's voice broke into her consciousness. "I still say I can't believe you two are sisters!" he exclaimed. Standing there by the table, he drank his Coke quickly. "Denne, let's dance," he said, when he had finished it. "I love this song," he went on, "and surely you don't have to work all the time."

Reluctantly Denne prepared to leave her haven. She turned to the girl at the other end of the long table. "Glenda, can you manage the drinks in addition to the food for a little while?"

"Sure, Denne, go ahead and dance."

"I'll be back in just a little while," Denne promised loudly, more for Reece's benefit than Glenda's.

Unfortunately Reece had chosen a slow song and Denne spent the entire dance trying to stay as far away from him as possible. When the music finally stopped, she saw that she and Reece were standing on the edge of a group made up of Michael, Alicia, Brad, Kathy, and two other couples whom Denne barely knew.

"Well, look where we are," Reece exclaimed. "Here's the queen. Why don't you introduce me, Denne?"

"Uh, she's busy right now," Denne stammered, "and I really need to be getting back. . . ."

Before she could finish the sentence Michael saw her. His smile went straight to Denne's heart, and when he put his arm around her to draw them into the group she thought she'd never be able to breathe again.

"Denne, hi! Are you having a good time?" he asked.

Denne avoided answering his question by introducing Reece to him and to Kathy.

"We'll introduce you to the others in just a minute, Reece," Michael promised. "They seem to be all involved in some deep discussion at the moment," he said.

Denne followed his eyes to Alicia, who although

she was surrounded by five people, obviously was aware of no one but Brad. She was laughing up into his deep blue eyes that almost exactly matched her own, the long slim fingers of one of her hands resting lightly on his arm.

Denne turned to see Michael's reaction to that scene, but when she looked up at him she found that he was no longer looking at Alicia. His attentive look was fastened on her face.

15

School on Monday was a great relief for Denne. She walked into the building eager to get to class and to work—to get her mind back into her studies and off her social life and the disastrous homecoming weekend. She went to her locker for the morning's supply of books and as soon as she saw the Shakespeare text she remembered that she was supposed to finish reading *As You Like It* for Mrs. Ulrich's class today. She hurried to homeroom and as soon as she was seated flipped open the book and started skimming the last act.

When the bell rang she left homeroom and went straight to her seat in English class hoping to go over at least a few more pages before class began. She had just opened the book when Mrs. Ulrich's voice at her elbow startled her.

"Denne, I'm glad you're here a little early. I've been wanting to talk with you," she said.

"Yes, Mrs. Ulrich?"

"Mme Clouet tells me that you were in a play this past summer and that you did very well," the English teacher said.

Denne was surprised that the teachers had been discussing her. "Well, yes, I was in *Can-Can* and I loved it."

"Why don't you try out for a part in *As You Like It?* It would really enrich your Shakespeare studies and I'm sure you'd have a lot of fun doing it. Have you considered it at all?"

"Yes, I've been thinking about it," Denne replied.

"Casting for the female roles will be done Thursday afternoon after school," Mrs. Ulrich told her. "I was thinking that you might like to try for the part of Celia, but if there's another part you'd like, feel free to try for it, of course." Mrs. Ulrich began to move down the aisle toward her desk. "I really hope you'll be there, Denne."

All during class Denne had a warm feeling of returning self-confidence. Mrs. Ulrich thought she could get a part in the play, Mme Clouet had evidently said some good things about her—I can do it in spite of everything, she thought. I can build my own separate identity. This play is something I can excel in, and it'll have nothing to do with Alicia because she's already said that she doesn't have time for it.

The idea of being in the play grew more and more important to Denne as the day went on. She had trouble concentrating in every class except English because she was constantly trying to unobtrusively look at the text of the play and decide which part she'd like. They had gone over the first act in English class and Celia seemed all right for her, but she kept thinking of Michael's words, "You just go right into those tryouts and try for the leading role." Rosalind looked like an interesting part, and it would be fun to be the star again.

By the time she was to meet Michael for their first session of the week, Denne had decided on Rosalind. She smiled in anticipation of telling him, remembering the mock sternness in his voice when he told her to try out. He really cares whether I try out or not, she thought, and he believes I can get the part.

Michael was waiting, his book open in front of him. He looked up when Denne came into the room, a welcoming smile on his face.

"You look a little bit different from the last time I saw you," he teased. "I was expecting a glamorous girl in a long red dress instead of a teacher in corduroy."

"Could that be because you don't want to do any work today?" Denne laughed.

"Well, maybe," he admitted, chuckling.

"You might as well expect the teacher in corduroy all the time; the girl in the red dress won't be appearing again soon," Denne said, suddenly serious.

"Why not?" Michael's voice held that quick interest once more. The interest in his voice and the concern in his eyes swept away all Denne's defenses, and brought her deepest feelings to the surface.

"I had the most miserable time," she blurted. "For once I had a date, but he didn't even know I existed. He didn't want to talk to me or to be with me—I couldn't even get his attention, much less keep it."

"Well, then he must be a clod," Michael stated flatly.

"Clod or no, I'm not saying 'yes' to another date for a long time, maybe never," Denne said.

Michael gave her a long look. "You shouldn't blame yourself if Saturday was a flop, Denne. It was his fault."

"No matter whose fault it was it has made me see that I'm not the belle of the ball; I can't handle a social life. I'm giving up dating and concentrating on other things from now on," Denne declared, opening her book and getting a pen from her purse.

"Like what?" he asked.

"Acting, for one thing," she replied.

Michael's white teeth flashed in his irresistible grin. "So you're following my orders, are you? Which part are you trying for? Is it the lead?"

"Well, of course. You don't think I'd disobey you, do you?" Denne smiled, looking up into his dark eyes.

"I certainly hope not. Now you just go in there and get that part and when the play is produced you'll feel a lot different about yourself, you just wait and see," he told her.

Denne pulled her eyes away from his and looked down at the book. *"Qu'avez-vous perdu?"* she began.

"J'ai perdu mon livre," Michael answered quickly.

Well, I may not be any good on dates, she thought, but I must be a pretty good teacher. Michael's French is getting better in a hurry.

They had just managed to finish the entire exercise when the time was up.

"I've got to run; the coach'll be sore if I'm late," Michael said, gathering his books.

"Not so fast," Denne replied, tearing a sheet from her small notebook to write his assignments on. "You're not getting away without your homework."

"O.K." Michael sat patiently watching her refer to the book and then jot exercise numbers down on the paper. "When's the big day for tryouts?" he asked.

"Thursday after school," Denne answered absently, erasing one number and substituting another.

"Are we going to skip that session, then, or what?" Michael asked getting up and reaching for the piece of paper in her hand.

"Oh, I forgot that would conflict with us," she said, as his fingers closed over hers and lingered for a moment. A delicious thrill moved through her and she sat very still, unable to raise her eyes to his. His hand was hard and strong; Denne wanted it to stay on hers forever. For a long moment he didn't move either. Then he took the assignment sheet and slipped it into his textbook.

Denne swallowed and managed to find her voice. "We'll have to make the session up, but I know we can't use this room on Friday. Assuming you can meet on Friday." At last she was able to look at him.

He was standing in front of her, very tall and broad-shouldered, so handsome she thought she could not bear it. Her eyes moved to his big tanned hand holding the stack of books so easily against his blue-jeaned thigh. It seemed strange to look at it there when she could still feel it against hers.

"Friday is fine with me," he was saying. "Why don't we just meet at your house? Do you think your mom would mind?"

The thought of being with Michael someplace besides this impersonal classroom made her feel weak.

"I . . . no, I don't think she'd mind," she said, surprised that her voice didn't tremble. "What time?"

"How about our usual time, right after school?" he asked. "In fact, you could just ride home with Alicia and me. We'll take her to cheerleading practice, then go home and get right to work. Listen, I've really got to run now, see you Friday, O.K.?" Michael moved quickly toward the door. He opened it, then turned with a broad smile on his face. "Good luck at tryouts, Denne. I'll be pulling for you," he said, and was gone.

Denne sat at her desk for a long time remembering Michael's touch. She closed her eyes and imagined that his fingers were still closed around hers, wishing that he was still with her. The excitement was still so strong that it made her feel weak all over. I meant what I told him except for one thing, she thought. If he were the one who asked me for a date there's no way I could say no.

All day Thursday Denne vacillated between panic and self-assurance. Fortunately when she walked into the auditorium after school self-assurance was uppermost. Mrs. Ulrich, Mrs. Henderson, and Mr. Sloane were sitting in the front row of seats on the right side and Mrs. Ulrich motioned for Denne to come over to them. She handed Denne a clipboard that held a list of parts with blanks under each one.

"Please sign the list, Denne, and then be seated in the center section," she said. "When your name is called you may read from scene 3 of Act I; we're trying candidates for Celia and Rosalind at the same time."

Denne sat down on a row by herself so she could concentrate and started to look over that scene. She kept thinking how surprised Mrs. Ulrich would be when she read for Rosalind instead of for Celia. For just a moment she hesitated. Maybe I should read for Celia, she thought. Mrs. Ulrich isn't the only one who thinks of me as the best-friend-of-the-star type —everyone else in the English speaking world does, too. I might do a much better job in a role that matches my regular personality.

Denne straightened up, determined. In the French-speaking world last summer, though, I was definitely the star, she thought, and I can be again. On the stage I'll be Rosalind, not Denne, and I can do anything. Maybe I can even change the way Clinton High sees me; after this play they'll have to see me in a new light!

Michael's voice sounded in her mind, "when the play is produced you'll feel a lot different about yourself" he'd said. He must already see me in some different way, she thought. But there's no one else here at Clinton who would think I should try for the lead. Oh, face it, Denne, she scolded herself. He's just trying to make you feel better, after all, you are always whining and feeling sorry for yourself when he's there to listen. He doesn't see you as a star, he sees you as a basket case! The thought that maybe Michael was just feeling sorry for her was so painful that Denne forced her mind from him onto the book in front of her. Her eyes fell on Rosalind's speech to her uncle as he banished her, and her lips moved silently.

"I do beseech your Grace.
Let me the knowledge of my fault bear with
me. . . ."

Stubbornly, her thoughts went back to Michael. He *does* really think I can do this, she said in a whisper. I didn't just imagine the caring look in his eyes or the concern in his voice, I know I didn't.

Denne's reverie was broken by Mrs. Ulrich. She had taken her place as director on the stage and was calling for quiet in the big room.

"It is time to begin the tryouts for Rosalind and for Celia. I will call the names in the order that they are here on the registration sheet, and you will take your places on the stage and read from Act I, scene 3." She glanced at the clipboard in her hand. "Carolyn Bookman to read for Celia and Linda Lewis to read for Rosalind," she announced.

Carolyn and Linda rose from their seats directly in front of Denne and started down the aisle to the stage. Denne looked them over appraisingly. She didn't know either girl, she had no way of knowing how much competition Linda would be.

The reading began and Denne relaxed. Linda obviously had little or no stage experience—her voice barely projected as far back as Denne's seat, and she stumbled over two words in one line. I know I can get the part, Denne thought. I just know I can! She started going over the lines in earnest, really getting up for her turn.

A small disturbance at the side front of the

auditorium drew Denne's attention. The door there was just closing, at first she didn't see who had come through it. Then she noticed that two girls were bending over whispering to Mr. Sloane. There was no mistaking the blond hair catching the light from the stage. It was Alicia. Both girls straightened up and moved to find seats and Denne saw that it was Julie with her.

Denne's fingers froze around her book; her chest hurt so that she could hardly breathe. But she said she wasn't going to try out! she silently cried,feelings of betrayal and dismay and frustration churning inside her. She told me herself that she did not have time to be in the play and now here she is!

Linda and Carolyn finished their reading and left the stage. Mr. Sloane called, "We have two more prospective actresses here, Mrs. Ulrich. They want to try for Rosalind and Celia, too."

Mrs. Ulrich looked at Alicia and Julie and nodded, jotting their names down on her list. "Susan McCarthy for Celia and Patty Arnold for Rosalind," she called.

Denne sat, close to tears. I can't do this, she thought. For one thing I cannot get up on that stage and try out in front of Alicia and for another thing I cannot stand it when she gets the part. She doesn't even have time to do this, and she'll be the star. *I'm* the one who needs it! Denne's fists clenched. It would be just like Mrs. Ulrich to ask me again to read for Celia, she thought. She'd think that was just perfect—Alicia for Rosalind and me playing her best friend. Denne felt the blood rush to her face with the thought.

Denne closed her copy of the play and stacked her books on her lap. When Mrs. Ulrich turned to show

Susan and Patty where to stand on the stage and to start them on their reading, Denne stood up and moved as quietly as possible into the aisle. She turned and walked swiftly toward the doors in the back expecting every second to hear Mrs. Ulrich or Mr. Sloane call after her. Thankfully, she reached the double doors and slipped through them into the lobby.

Her throat felt as if she were choking, but she couldn't stop to calm herself. She strode across the lobby and into the main hallway desperate for the outside air. Pushing blindly through the door onto the front steps her shoulder bumped hard into the chest of a tall boy who was coming in.

"I'm sorry," she muttered.

"That's O.K.," he answered. "Say, are you coming from play tryouts?"

She nodded.

"I'm supposed to pick Alicia up. Alicia Drake. Has she tried out yet?"

Instantly Denne's glance shot to his face. It was Brad Fitzgerald.

"N-no, not yet," she stammered.

"O.K., thanks," he replied, disappearing into the building.

Denne stood unmoving on the top step. *Brad* was supposed to pick Alicia up? Brad? So she's making progress, Denne thought bitterly. She'll have him wrapped around her finger before he knows what hit him, and without a doubt she'll manage to keep Michael, too.

Her feet moved hesitantly down one step at a time, her mind spinning. It isn't fair, it just is not fair. She won't leave me in peace in one thing I try to do; everywhere I turn there she is or if she isn't there, someone is talking about her. She dates the only boy I want in this entire school, and now she's adding another guy to her collection. She is the main topic of conversation at the meetings of *my* committees, she is the reason people want to make friends with me, she is the eternal standard that people judge me by, everybody from Aunt Edith to my one and only blind date, and now in the one activity that I might be really good at she had to step in and take my role.

Denne walked disconsolately under the enormous elm trees on Evans Road without seeing them. The wind stirred the branches, taking a few more leaves each time. Denne's brown loafers crunched through them, but she didn't hear the crisp sound.

By the time she reached home she was furious, not only with Alicia, but with herself. There go all my good intentions, she thought, all my plans for becoming an independent celebrity. How can I ever hope to succeed at that when all I do is run away? There's no way I can reach goals if I don't even try. She stormed up the stairs to her room thankful that her mother wasn't there. I don't know how I'll ever explain this to her, she thought miserably. She'll be here in a few minutes asking for all the details about tryouts and what I think my chances are.

Denne dropped her things on the desk and kicked her shoes into opposite corners of the room. Even worse, how will I explain this to Michael? He honestly believed I would get that part and I didn't even try.

Denne threw herself across her bed and sobbed.

16

The delicious aroma of spice cookies greeted Denne as soon as she opened the door on Friday afternoon.

"Denne?" her mother called from the kitchen.

"Yes, Mom," she answered, dropping her books and coat on the chair in the hall and then picking through them for her French books and notebook.

"I see you're fighting the November blahs with your usual baking spree," she said as she entered the kitchen.

Margaret glanced up from the cookie sheet she'd just taken from the oven. "I could hardly believe it was you; I thought you were riding with Michael and Alicia today," she said.

"I was, but Alicia had to go pick up her new cheerleading sweater and I just didn't want to hang around with them that long," she replied, reaching for a golden-brown cookie.

Margaret glanced at her closely, but all she said was, "I didn't know where you and Michael would want to work so I haven't set up a table or anything, but I've built a fire in the den. It's such a gray day I thought that'd be cheerful."

Denne munched the cookie. "I don't know how cheerful today can be, but maybe that'll help," she said gloomily.

"What's wrong, Denne?" Margaret's voice and eyes were filled with concern as she stopped dropping cookie batter and gave her full attention to her daughter. "Are you this disappointed about not getting a part in the play?"

"It's nothing, Mom," Denne evaded her question and her inquiring look. "I'd better go on in and get a table set up, Michael will be here soon."

Denne had just put her books on the couch and was crossing the room to the closet for the card table when the doorbell rang. "I'll get it," she called toward the kitchen.

Michael was standing on the steps, his stack of books held easily in one big hand. He and Denne said hello, and he followed her down the hall sniffing the air. "Your mom must be baking again," he said hopefully. "Suppose she'll offer us some sustenance to get us through all this work?"

Denne smiled. "You know how she is, Michael. She'll be in there stuffing cookies down us; she loves to have people eat what she cooks."

Denne put Michael's coat away and started getting out the table.

"Oh, let's not use that," he said. "We don't have that much writing to do. Let's just sit here on the couch so we can watch the fire." Michael sat down, piling his books on the floor at his feet, "Hey, this is great," he said. "Let's meet here all the time, O.K.?"

"Umm, O.K.," Denne answered absentmindedly. She settled herself on the couch and started looking for the right page in her textbook.

Michael held his on his lap, but didn't open it. "I don't feel like studying today," he said, stretching his long legs toward the fire. "I just want to be lazy."

Denne smiled ruefully. "I don't feel lazy, but I don't want to work either," she informed him, chewing on her pencil, then running it through her dark curls, her eyes on the dancing yellow flames in the hearth.

Michael looked at her steadily. "All the way to cheerleading practice Alicia was talking about being in the play," he said. "How did tryouts go for you?"

Denne looked up at him quickly, a sharp excitement running through her at the way he had read her thoughts.

"I . . . I," she began, then stopped as Margaret came into the room with a plate of cookies and two Cokes.

"Hello, Michael," she said, putting the tray on the coffee table. "I hope you like these cookies; they're a new recipe."

"Hello, Mrs. Drake," he answered. "I'm sure I will, I always like everything you cook."

"Well, you all get a lot done, now," she said. "That scholarship test will be here before you know it."

When Margaret had left the room, Michael turned to Denne again, all attention.

"I haven't told my mom this," she said quietly,

"but I didn't stay to try out. I left before it was my turn to read. When she asked me how I did, I just told her I didn't get a part." Denne stuck her pencil into her open book, twisted one brown curl in her fingers and looked down at her book.

"Why didn't you read? I thought you were all excited about being in the play," Michael's voice was indignant. "I just know you would have gotten a part."

Denne couldn't raise her eyes to his face. "I wouldn't have, though," she said in a low tone. "At least not the lead. Alicia came in and I knew the lead would go to her."

"No, you didn't," Michael said. "You didn't know that until the casting was done."

Denne looked up at him, her wide eyes shiny with suppressed tears, her voice shaking with indignation. "I *did* know it! Is there anything at all that she ever wanted that she didn't get?"

Michael's eyes held hers with a mixture of concern and exasperation. "You could get anything you wanted, too, you know," he stated firmly. "All you have to do is believe in yourself a little bit." He handed her a Coke and took the other can of pop and a cookie from the tray in front of them.

Denne sipped at the sweet liquid, the carbonation stinging her throat. "Michael, I can't. Not while everyone sees me only as Alicia's little sister. I wouldn't have had a chance at the lead, because all the teachers automatically see Alicia as the lead, the star. I might have been cast as Celia, her best friend, but there's no way I could have overcome the way the whole world has me typed enough to get the part of Rosalind. Not with my sister in the running."

She waved away the cookies he offered her and

continued to talk, the words pouring from her uncontrollably. "I've decided that I'll just have to stay in the world I'm good at—my studies, and forget about activities as well as dating. As long as Alicia and I are in the same school I can't move out of her shadow." She took another drink of Coke and tapped the can impatiently against the edge of the French book. "Every activity I get into it's Alicia this and Alicia that and even when I have a stupid blind date all the guy can see is Alicia and I'm tired of it."

Michael finished his cookie and turned toward Denne, his arm stretched out on the back of the couch behind her. "You ought to forget about Alicia and just do your own thing," he said. "You have a lot of talent that Alicia doesn't have and you are a pretty interesting person in your own right, but nobody will know that if you run away from such things as tryouts."

"Well, if that's true, you're the only person I know who can see it," she answered. "I didn't want to run away, but I just could not face another round of being compared to her and coming up short! I want to have some recognition of my own, and I've realized the only way to do that is to really work hard in my studies and forget about everything else."

Absentmindedly, Michael twirled one of Denne's curls that was touching his fingers on the back of the couch. He shook his head. "Then you're running away again," he told her firmly, tilting her head to look into her eyes. "You can't hide in your books forever, you know."

A sharp electricity flashed through Denne. His touch, the look in his eyes, the caring tones of his voice all combined to catch her up and carry her into a magic world. She sat for long moments gazing into his brown eyes so alive with concern for her and interest in her problems and determination and something else that Denne didn't understand. He's different today, she thought. He's never been exactly like this before, but I'm not sure what is different. He's been interested and concerned before when I told him my problems, but there's something else in him today.

All of Denne's thoughts stopped as Michael's lips came down on hers. They were warm and tender and very, very gentle as they kissed her softly and then moved away. Their touch reminded her of the look in his eyes. He's telling me in another way that he really cares when I'm hurt, she thought. He's feeling sorry for me again.

Nevertheless, the marvelous sensation of his mouth on hers filled Denne with joy, with a desire to float away into a world that held only the two of them. Oh, I wish he'd kiss me again, she thought, and not because he feels sorry for me, either.

Denne didn't know how long they sat on the couch, apart, yet held very close together by Michael's strong arm and the look that passed between them. At last he pulled his eyes away from hers and moved his hand from her hair to his book.

"We'd better get going on this," he said huskily. "Your mom is right; it won't be long until test time."

Denne woke to her mother's voice. "Denne, Denne, it's time to get up." She opened her eyes a tiny bit and through her sleepy haze saw Margaret sitting on the foot of her bed.

"I hate to wake you on Saturday, dear, but it's

almost noon and I'm in the mood to go somewhere and have lunch before I go shopping; I'd like to make a day of it. Why don't you come with me?"

Denne rubbed her eyes and stretched, then stifled a yawn. She pulled the warm quilts up around her shoulders and settled into her pillows cozily.

"Oh, Mom, I wish I could," she said, "but I simply have to stay in and work on the skit for the French Club Variety Show. It sounds like fun, though."

Margaret bristled. "Listen, Denne, you are working much too hard. For the past three weeks you have done absolutely nothing except go to school, study, tutor and work on this skit. You hardly even take time to talk to Sharon on the phone, much less to see her. You aren't eating enough nor sleeping enough and if you keep it up you'll be sick."

"I won't get sick, Mom, I promise," Denne smiled at her from the comfortable depths of her bed. "I'll stay in bed while I work and that'll be resting and getting something done at the same time." She glanced at the clipboard full of papers and the pen on the floor near her. "That's what I did last night until I fell asleep."

Margaret shook her head determinedly. "No, that isn't resting. You need some recreation. I'll take you out to lunch, we'll shop for clothes for a while and then you can come back and work some more. Is it tonight that Jeff's coming over to help you with it?"

"Yes, and I really need to have the entire rough draft done before he gets here, Mom," Denne pleaded. "I can't do that if I go shopping. We're trying to do an imitation of Molière, and that takes a lot of time."

Margaret was looking off into the distance as if she

weren't listening. "You know, Denne, I've been thinking about Jeff. He's been around quite a bit since you have been collaborating in this writing project, and I've noticed that he really likes you. Why don't you go out with him? In fact, he'd be a good date for the Winter Dinner Dance. Do you realize that's coming up in just a few weeks?"

Denne's heart sank at the suggestion. One of the reasons she was working so hard was to try to keep her thoughts off Michael and how much she would like to go to the big dance with him. The twice-weekly tutoring sessions were the highlight of her weeks; she could still feel the mysterious new element that had come into their relationship that day in the den, but outwardly nothing had changed and she couldn't understand what was different. Whatever it was, he was not asking her for dates except in her dreams.

"I know, Mom, I just don't think I want to go with Jeff," she answered, restlessly throwing back the covers and sitting up.

"Why not?" Margaret persisted. "He's a nice boy and I know that he is attracted to you."

"Maybe so," Denne answered as she searched around with her feet for her house shoes, "but I'm interested in him only as a friend. Besides, I've given up dating and all that kind of thing; I'm no good at it anyway."

She slipped into the moccasins and reached for the tailored navy flannel robe on the back of her chair. "I'll go with you for a while, Mom, if we can be back by four or so. I guess it would be a pretty long day sitting around here by myself."

She felt Margaret's eyes on her back as she padded out of her room to take a shower.

17

Dressed and ready to go, Denne came downstairs to find her mother waiting for Alicia to get off the phone.

"I want to find out her plans for the day and tell her ours," Margaret explained, "but I can't catch her awake and off the phone at the same time. I think, though, that she's about to hang up at last."

Alicia's silky voice was purring into the phone in tones that seemed to indicate the end of the conversation. "All right, Brad," she was saying, "I'll be ready at 2:00. Bye now."

Alicia hung up and turned to her mother and sister. "You two look all dressed up and ready for the day. Where are you going?"

"Out to lunch and shopping," Margaret answered. "I don't suppose you'd have time to join us?"

Alicia smiled, shaking her head in mock regret. "No, I'm afraid I don't—I'm going skating with Brad this afternoon and to a movie with Michael this evening, and I have to do my hair."

"Are you and Brad beginning to date often?" Margaret asked as she went to the closet for her coat. "What does Michael think about that? You aren't breaking up with him, are you?"

"No, Mom," Alicia said quickly, moving toward the stairs. "We've decided that it'll be good for both of us to date other people occasionally."

"Well, I think you're right," Margaret said firmly, drawing on her gloves. "I've always said that high school is too young to tie yourself down to one person."

Margaret chattered happily during the drive into Lewisville through the crisp bright morning. Denne tried her best to concentrate on the conversation, but her thoughts kept going back to Alicia's plans for the day—dates with the two best-looking boys at Clinton High, and both in the same day! She didn't care about Brad, but she would give anything if she could be the one with Michael tonight.

Margaret parked the car with a flourish on Lewisville's busy Main Street. Denne looked up and saw with surprise that they were directly in front of her favorite restaurant, Le Château.

"Mom!" she exclaimed. "This is much too expensive for a shopping lunch! I didn't know when you said you were taking me to lunch that you meant this!"

"I think that a person who has been slaving over a French play for weeks should have a lovely lunch at a French restaurant as a reward," Margaret said with a smile. "Come on now, let's enjoy the marvelous food and then hit every store in town!"

Le Château was quiet and dark, elegant with its small tables covered in white linen, a single rose in a crystal vase on every table. Denne had been there twice before but she was as thrilled as she had been the first time; the quiet atmosphere and the elegant food made her feel she was not only sampling another culture, but entering another world as well. She ordered a quiche and strawberry crêpes for dessert, then sat back in her chair to smile gratefully at her mother.

"As usual, Mrs. Drake, you have accomplished your purpose," she said. "I already feel relaxed and rested and ready to forget about work so I can get serious about shopping!"

Denne's leisurely mood increased as they enjoyed the food and planned which stores to visit. For the first time in several weeks she forgot completely about school and all her problems; she let herself become absorbed in Margaret's plans for her own wardrobe and Denne's.

"You really need some new tops for school, Denne, and maybe a couple of skirts," Margaret smiled at her daughter over coffee. "And a dressy outfit of some kind—all you have is school-type clothes."

"But Mom, I really don't need anything dressy," she protested, visions of new designer jeans floating in her head. "I don't go out that much."

"You will very soon, though," Margaret answered, gathering up her purse and pushing back her chair. "You'll be dating Jeff or some of the other boys if you'll give them a little encouragement!"

Denne's mood was ruined. Her stomach tensed at

the thoughts of dating and of Michael which always seemed to be linked in her mind these days. As she and Margaret stepped out into the cold outside air and walked toward The Toggery she tried to recapture her earlier relaxation but she was beginning to suspect that the pressure from Margaret about her social life was going to continue. That would keep Michael uppermost in her mind and she could not bear to visualize him out with Alicia on their usual Saturday night date.

"Let's shop for you first, Mom," she said, hoping to divert Margaret from the painful subject.

"Oh, we'll get to me soon enough," her mother answered, holding the wide glass door open for Denne. "Here's the junior shop right here; let's check it out first."

As soon as they walked into the section of the store called the Bird's Nest Denne knew that she was in for a whole afternoon of just what she wanted to avoid. There, in the middle of the shop on a dark-haired mannequin, was a long dress that both Margaret and Denne recognized as being just made for Denne. Margaret gasped and stopped short, pulling at Denne's arm to make her stand beside her.

"Look, darling, look at that dress. It is absolutely you!" Her eyes moved over the simple lines of the velveteen, imagining Denne in the mannequin's place.

Denne knew immediately that her mother was right. The color was a jewellike navy blue, Denne's favorite, and the simple way the dress was cut made it fit into the tailored style that Denne always bought. It was very dressy, too, though, very much an evening dress.

"You must try it on right now, before we do

anything else!" Margaret stated emphatically. "That is the dress you must have for the Winter Dinner Dance; nothing else will do." She began looking around and signaling to a clerk.

Denne shrank away from the clerk's gaze, uncomfortable and indignant. "Mom," she whispered furiously, "forget it. I don't even have a date for the Winter Dinner Dance. Why in the world should I have a dress for it?"

Margaret acted as if she hadn't spoken as the clerk approached them. "We'd like to try that dress, please," she said, "I think a size 5 will be fine."

"We only have the one," the clerk answered. "Let me check the size."

She came back from the desk in a moment and started undressing the mannequin. "This one happens to be a 5, ma'am, you're in luck."

Denne was silent as the three of them went back to the dressing room, the dress draped over the clerk's arm. As soon as the woman was gone, however, she burst out, "Why should I try on this dress, Mom? Why? I'll just fall in love with it and there's no point in buying it because I'll never have a chance to wear it! I'm not planning to attend the wonderful Winter Dinner Dance!" Her lips trembled with indignation.

Margaret faced her, astonished at the vehemence in Denne's tone. Her own voice was filled with surprise. "But, Denne, of course you will! Someone will ask you to it if you'll only let them! Why Jeff would take you in a minute!" Nervously she began to unzip the dress. "You can't just skip it, that's one of the most important events of the entire school year; it's something that all your classmates will share and you don't want to miss out on it."

Denne sank onto the small chair in the corner of the dressing room and when she raised her eyes to her mother's they were filled with tears. "I don't want to go with Jeff, Mother," she said softly, her voice breaking. "I wanted this to be a really special occasion."

Margaret looked at her steadily for a long moment. "It can be, Denne, no matter who is your date. The key to that is your own attitude."

Her throat so tight she couldn't answer, Denne stood up, kicked off her loafers and slowly began to remove her jeans and red sweater. She stood in front of the long mirror in her bra and panties and Margaret slipped the soft folds of velveteen over her head. She zipped up the back and Denne stared into the wide brown eyes of an entirely new person. The dark color brought out the deep lights in her eyes and her rich brown hair and made her skin look like pale cream. The neckline was high and plain, but the sleeveless armholes were cut ever so slightly high on the shoulders, giving the dress a sophisticated, slightly sexy look. Denne swallowed hard.

"I love it," she managed to say.

"So do I, it's perfect for you," Margaret replied.

The clerk reappeared at the door of the dressing room. "How'd it do?" she asked.

"We'll take it," Margaret answered, giving the glamorous Denne a hug.

The rest of the shopping trip went well; Denne got one pair of designer jeans and a long-sleeved knit top, and Margaret bought a dress. They returned to the car at last, tired but happy with the day. Denne settled herself in her seat for the drive back to Clinton, closing her eyes and propping her head on her folded jacket. She kept seeing herself in the beautiful blue dress, and her mind began to open just a tiny crack to the idea that she might go to the dance with Jeff after all. Every time, she thought that however, her emotions overcame and insisted that Michael should be her date. The dress, though, the dress, she told them silently. A dress like that shouldn't be wasted. The turmoil inside her was worse than ever, she thought. Her dream for a whole year had been to go to the Winter Dinner Dance with Michael and she had always known that if she couldn't go with him she just wouldn't go at all. Now she had to think of other possibilities because she wanted so badly to wear that dress and to at least let him see her in it whether he was her date or not.

But Jeff! Jeff would interpret a date to the biggest event of the season as practically a declaration of love, she thought. He certainly would not expect to go with her to that and then never date her again. She twisted her hair and squirmed restlessly.

She looked over at Margaret quiet behind the wheel, her eyes on the road.

"Mom?"

"Yes, dear?"

"I think you are a craftier lady than even I have ever thought."

Margaret gave her an inquiring glance. "Why do you say that?"

"Because when you decide a person should have a social life you certainly know how to motivate her into getting one."

Margaret smiled, her eyes crinkling at the edges. "Denne, I'm afraid I don't know what you're talking about," she said, laughter in her voice.

18

Monday afternoon Denne plumped the pillows on the couch and stirred the fire in preparation for Michael's tutoring session. She was having to fight more and more now to keep her mind on school work and French Club and away from the brown-eyed boy who was still dating her sister. His face floated into her thoughts at random times, and every time she looked at the velveteen dress a sharp pang of longing went through her. If only he would ask her to the dance! She sank onto the couch, hugging a pillow to her, staring into the fire. *I'd never want anything else again,* she thought. *If only I could go to the Winter Dinner Dance with Michael, I'd never want anything else.*

The memory of their kiss came back to her as it had a thousand times, and she relived the sweet sensation of his lips on hers. *I know he was just* feeling sorry for me, she told herself silently, he always cares so much about my feelings. That's all it was and I have to stop thinking about him this way or I'll be sitting here alone with my new dress when the Winter Dinner Dance rolls around. Maybe Jeff will ask me to go with him if I'll give him half a chance.

Michael's voice startled her. "Hi, Denne," he said. "You look too comfortable to do any work."

Denne looked up to see his tall form, a frosting of snow making his hair even lighter, holding his books and a square package wrapped in Christmas paper, a big red bow on top. She sat up straight and twisted around to look over the back of the couch.

"Well, you are certainly a surprise! I didn't hear the doorbell or anything," she greeted him.

"Your mom was going out as I came in," he explained. "She said to tell you that she's running next door to Mrs. Baxter's with some pumpkin bread; she'll be back as soon as she can get away."

Denne smiled. "That'll probably be next week. Mrs. Baxter really likes to talk."

She glanced at the package as he dropped it and his books on the end of the couch. "I thought this Thursday was Thanksgiving, not Christmas," she remarked. "Alicia isn't here right now, she's staying over tonight at Julie's so they can study."

"This isn't for Alicia," Michael said firmly. "This package is for you, my faithful teacher." His eyes gleamed with teasing and with something else Denne couldn't identify.

Denne's eyes opened wide, her heart skipped. Michael had brought a gift for her! She couldn't believe that he had actually bought a present and had it wrapped especially for her!

"You can't open it now," he continued, the teasing in his voice as well as his eyes. "When the work is all done we'll have a little party and celebrate Christmas a month early."

Denne chuckled. "O.K., but this is a switch. Usually I'm the taskmaster, not you."

They opened their books to get down to work, but even as Denne asked the first questions of the conversational exercise, *"Qui était Charlemagne? Quand a-t-il vécu?"* her eyes strayed to the bright red and green and white package. Her mind whirled. What did this mean? Had he been thinking of a surprise for her these past few weeks when his eyes had seemed to hold a secret she couldn't fathom?

Denne struggled to concentrate on the work; Michael showed that he had prepared well. In fact, she thought, he was actually improving so much that he might not need tutoring second semester. The sudden thought of not seeing him for these sessions gave Denne a sharp emptiness deep inside. She pushed the idea away, forcing her mind back to the page in front of her.

At last they had covered all the material and Denne made Michael's assignment for the next meeting. "This will be due a week from today since Thursday is a holiday," she told him, handing him the slip of paper and feeling again the warm thrill when his fingers touched hers.

"And speaking of holidays . . ." he said, "and lessons and assignments, remember when you were wishing that we had some maps of European countries in French so we could do some geography exercises?" Michael reached to take the heavy square package, lifted it and placed it in her lap.

"Well, here you are, *Mademoiselle la Maîtresse,* the maps and lots more information besides."

Denne carefully loosened the tape and lifted the heavy foil paper with the sprightly bow still attached. On her knees was a large dictionary. She gasped delightedly.

"Michael! A *Petit Larousse!*" Her eyes flew to his and the warmth she found there caught and held her in a glow of happiness. She looked into Michael's dark eyes for an endless moment; they held hers with a power that wouldn't let them go. She became aware of Michael's arm stretched behind her on the back of the couch, his fingers barely brushing her hair. Denne couldn't move, she couldn't breathe, even the slightest movement would break a priceless spell. Michael was the one who moved—he cupped Denne's head with his big hand and somehow he was suddenly very close, the warm scent of him making her dizzy. Her eyes closed then, and she was lost to everything but the touch of his warm lips on hers. She floated in a thrilling warmth that spread to every inch of her body; nothing existed except this strong male creature who held her in his spell.

When Michael pulled his mouth from hers, Denne couldn't move. She felt dizzy and so weak that she laid her head against the back of the couch, unable to pull her eyes away from him.

He gazed back at her for a long moment, then reached for his books. He gave the *Larousse* a friendly thump and said huskily, "Hope you enjoy it." Before Denne could move or reply, he was gone.

For a long time Denne sat on the couch, absently listening to the fire crackling in the grate, her eyes on the doorway Michael had gone through. All her senses were reliving over and over again the beautiful feeling of his mouth on hers, his body so close, his hand strong in her hair. She didn't intend ever to move from that spot; if the kiss couldn't last forever, at least maybe the afterglow could.

Gradually, though, her mind began to function again. Over and over she thought, Michael kissed me again! He actually gave me a real kiss, and he wasn't feeling sorry for me, either! Just the thought made her dizzy again, and her breath caught in her throat. He likes me. He must; he isn't the type of person to kiss someone like that if he didn't really think she was special. She stroked the fat book that lay sunk in the cushion against her leg. He must feel the same way about me that I do about him, she thought, happiness rising inside her like one of the flames in the hearth.

Denne had trouble concentrating all day Tuesday—this time even French class was no exception. She managed to avoid Madame's eye most of the hour, and the one time she couldn't, she was able to answer the question, even though she made an error in pronunciation. When the last bell rang she tried to slip by Madame's desk with a nod and a smile, hoping to go to her locker and then start her walk home without having to talk to anyone. Mme Clouet, however, was in the mood to chat.

"Denise, un moment, s'il vous plaît," she called as Denne neared the door.

Denne turned back, and when she saw Madame pulling a stack of college catalogs and application forms from a basket on her desk she knew that this conference would take more than a moment. Mme

Clouet had questioned Denne about her college plans before, and now, it seemed, she was getting serious.

"The guidance counselor sent me some new information today, Denne," the teacher began after asking Denne to sit down near her. "There is a fabulous new scholarship which will be available at Briar Hill College beginning next year for students who major in French." Madame handed Denne the thin catalog, its artful black and white cover depicting an ancient ivy-covered building surrounded by enormous trees. "Now I don't know whether you are particularly interested in Briar Hill," she went on, "but this scholarship includes all tuition and books for four years, plus an expense-paid junior year in France."

Denne's eyes widened at the thought. Her junior year in France! What a dream-come-true! She began to listen very carefully.

"The recipient of the Sussman Scholarship, as it is called (in honor of the person who funded it) will be determined by examinations which will be given in October of the preceding year. That means your exam is less than a year away if you decide to compete." Mme Clouet's dark eyes were blazing with enthusiasm for the idea, and Denne smiled to herself at the thought of the protests she would hear if she announced that she wasn't interested. As if she had read her thoughts, Madame went on. "Though why you wouldn't be interested is impossible for me to imagine," she said. Briskly she shuffled through the stack of forms and gave several to Denne. "You need to look these over and begin filling them out. You have to give notice soon that you intend to take the exam!"

Denne took the forms and slipped them into the catalog. "Thank you, Mme Clouet," she smiled. "It does sound like a wonderful opportunity."

"It is that," the French teacher declared, "and I believe you have a good chance of winning it. However, you'll need to begin preparing soon—the examinations are extremely thorough—they cover language, literature and culture, and are both oral and written."

The idea of such a challenge exhilarated Denne. "It's for sure I'll get to use my new *Larousse,*" she said, "and I'll need to start reading like crazy. Madame, will you . . ."

"Make you a reading list?" her teacher smiled. "I'll have it ready for you next week when we come back from vacation," she promised.

Denne walked home through the bitter November dampness, her thoughts swinging between the idea of the scholarship at Briar Hill and Michael. My dreams of going to France to study could come true, she thought, and images of Notre Dame and the Eiffel Tower floated before her for a moment. Then they were blotted out by the same image that had wrecked her concentration all day: Michael's warm brown eyes and sweet kiss.

Denne had spent hours last evening reliving those magic minutes with Michael, but today each time she replayed them in her mind nagging questions began to come at her. What did this mean? Twice now he had kissed her. Did he really like her, had he noticed she was a girl and not just a French tutor and a little sister? Would he kiss her again? Would they ever be able to have just a regular study session any more? Would he ever ask her out? Would he possibly, at this thought Denne always shivered with excitement, would he ask her to go with him to the Winter Dinner Dance?

Cold reality blotted out that hope as soon as Denne admitted it to herself. Of course Michael would take Alicia to the dance just as he had done last year, she thought. Her practical side said immediately that she should be letting Jeff take her to the dance so she could at least wear her gorgeous dress. But I have time, she argued to herself. The dance is still almost three weeks away. I won't try to get a date with Jeff just yet.

Denne came down Evans Road and turned the corner to her house dreaming of being dressed in her new velveteen dress all ready for the dance, posing to have her picture taken on Michael's arm. Then she noticed the car in front of the door with Alicia leaning in from the passenger side, talking. At first she assumed that it was Michael, bringing her home as he often did. With a start, she realized that the car was not Michael's, then she recognized Brad's curly dark head leaning across the seat as he talked with Alicia.

Denne stopped short, oblivious to the wind which was steadily getting colder as the sun moved lower in the sky. A terrible thought struck her which chilled her much more than the wind could. Maybe Michael's just on the rebound, she thought, watching her sister's animated face as she talked with Brad. Maybe Alicia has hurt Michael so much that he's just looking for some comfort. Maybe he only kissed me as a substitute for her!

That would explain it all, but the idea was unbearable, and Denne pushed it firmly to the back of her mind, forcing her feet to move toward home and her sister.

Brad pulled away and Alicia met Denne on the steps leading up to the front door.

"Hi, Den," she greeted her happily. "How'd your day go?"

"Oh, all right, I guess," Denne answered, following Alicia into the hallway to hang up her coat.

"I can't believe it!" Margaret announced from the kitchen door. "Both my girls here at once—what a treat!" She disappeared again calling over her shoulder, "Both of you come to the sun porch for a cup of hot chocolate and let's talk over the day!"

The girls hung up their coats and dropped their books on the hall table, playing with Muffin as they all followed Margaret.

"You first, Denne," Alicia said as they settled into the comfortable floral patterned chairs, Muffin curled at Denne's feet. "What exciting thing has happened to you today?"

Just as she had done at school, Denne wrenched her mind from Michael and his kiss and the reason for it and forced it onto the conversation. Carefully she sipped at the hot liquid.

"Well, Mme Clouet told me about a really good scholarship to Briar Hill College—it would pay tuition and books plus it would include my junior year in France!" As she talked Denne got excited about the scholarship all over again.

"Denne, that's wonderful!" Margaret exclaimed, her needle moving in and out of her canvas, needlepointing even faster than usual.

"It won't be easy to get, though," Denne said. "The exams are really stiff and I'll have to begin preparing for them now."

"I'm sure you'll do very well," her mother assured her, "and even if you happened not to get the scholarship you would have learned a tremendous amount. That's a real challenge for you, Denne. I think you should try for it."

Alicia stretched languidly in her chair, the cup of chocolate cooling on the small table beside her. "That's a real coincidence," she drawled, playing with a strand of her long yellow hair. "I heard something about a scholarship today, too."

"Oh, what?" Margaret's blue eyes were round with surprise, since Alicia's grades had never been exactly what it takes to get an academic scholarship. "Tell us about it, 'Lish, what college is giving it?"

"The State University. They give tuition scholarships in leadership to ten students every year, and Mr. Monro told me today that he has entered my name. You have to be nominated by your high school principal." She took the cup and sipped at her drink. "They use some sort of point system—ten points for being president of a club, seven points for being in a play, you know, that kind of thing. Mr. Monro says that I have more points than anyone else at Clinton, and he really thinks I have a chance of being one of the ten chosen from the whole state." Alicia smiled. "Of course, I'm not too sure I want to go to State, but it would be nice to win."

"Well, since you haven't even decided on a major, I think you could go to State for a couple of years at least," Margaret said firmly. "It would certainly help with the family finances if your tuition were paid."

"Well, it just sort of depends on where some other people go," Alicia said, kicking off her shoes and tucking her feet under her. "I'd hate to go off somewhere all by myself."

Margaret glanced at her sharply. "Well, Michael is trying for a scholarship at McClintock if that's what you mean, but that is a very expensive school, Alicia."

Denne went cold inside. She had never thought of Alicia following Michael to McClintock.

"I wasn't thinking about Michael," Alicia said with a mysterious air. "I wasn't thinking of him at all."

Denne and Margaret looked at Alicia questioningly, but she just sipped her hot chocolate and smiled at them.

"Well, it seems things never change," Denne said, "you didn't even apply for your scholarship and I'm going to study for almost a year for mine." She tried to keep her voice light, but she wanted to burst into tears. She felt very tired from spending all day trying to figure out Michael's motives for two little kisses that probably meant nothing at all to him and here was Alicia, implying that she was already so involved with Brad that they were going to the same college. And she still can have Michael any time she wants him, any time at all, she thought. I'm a perfect fool for giving one minute of my day to even thinking about him because he'd still be crazy about Alicia no matter how she treated him.

Margaret gave Denne an understanding look. "But you just remember, Denne, you'll learn so much from all that studying—why you'll be speaking French like a native when you're through."

"I know you're right, Mom," Denne said softly. "Now I'm going up to my room and try to get some work done before it's time for dinner."

Monday afternoon after French class Denne managed to avoid another discussion with Madame, but Jeff latched onto her as she left the classroom and walked with her to her locker. "Where have you been lately?" he asked. "I've been wanting to talk with you, but you always rush away after class."

"I've just been really busy," she answered, standing in front of the gray metal door, trying to think of her combination. "I've had a lot of things on my mind, Jeff."

"Well," Jeff cleared his throat. "There's something on my mind, too, Denne. . . ." He hesitated. "There's something I've been intending to ask you. . . ."

Oh, no, here it comes! she thought. Her mind began racing rapidly around the problem she'd been over so many times before. What should I do? she thought frantically. Should I tell Jeff yes? Is this my only chance to go to the dance?

"Hey, Denne!" A shout floated down the hall, and they turned to see Michael's tall form loping toward them, his letter jacket slung over his shoulder. Excitement and a fierce shyness combined shot through Denne's entire body.

"Look, Denne, we'll talk about it later, O.K.?" Jeff muttered. "I've got to go now."

"O.K., 'bye," Denne answered, smiling as Jeff almost collided with Michael in his haste to leave. Her heart was thudding unbearably hard as Michael stopped very near her and propped his arm up against her locker, almost encircling her.

"Denne, I can't come to our session today," he said, looking down into her eyes. "We are having a meeting of the team to close out football season, and I have to be there; I didn't know anything about it until about an hour ago."

Denne felt she couldn't possibly speak around the

butterflies fluttering in her throat. Finally she managed, "It's all right, Michael, we'll make it up later."

"I know, but there was something I was going to ask you today," he answered. "In fact, I was going to ask you last time, but I didn't."

Denne looked up into his warm eyes; she could hardly hear what he was saying because his nearness was bringing back all the wonderful sensations of his kiss and for the thousandth time she was imagining the feel of his lips on hers.

"I know you said a while back that you were never going to date again," he was saying, "but I'm really hoping that you didn't mean that."

The word "date" startled her, and Denne started to listen carefully.

"You had a bad experience, but you could have a good date, you know," he went on. "I'd like to take you out and have a chance to change your attitude. Denne . . ." His big hand reached out to take one of her curls and wrap it around his finger. "Denne, will you go to the Winter Dinner Dance with me?"

Denne's eyes opened as wide as they could go and she stood very, very still, positive that she must have misunderstood him, yet at the same time knowing that he had actually said the words she had dreamed of hearing for an entire year. She looked into his face to confirm it, and the question in his smiling eyes drew the answer from her lips.

"Oh, yes, Michael, yes I will," she whispered, her voice suddenly as weak as her wobbly legs.

His white teeth flashed in a joyous grin. "That's great!" His arm dropped from the locker to her shoulders and he gave her a quick hug. "Talk to you later," he said and bounded away down the hall, smiling back at her over his shoulder.

Denne watched him disappear, then she leaned her blushing forehead against the cool metal of the locker and closed her eyes, afraid to open them again for fear the dream would disappear.

Finally she recovered enough to gather the books she needed. She threaded her way through the students in the hall to the main door, saying I can't believe it! over and over again to herself. I'm actually going to have my dream come true! I, Denne Drake, am going to the Winter Dinner Dance with Michael Long! I am perfectly happy—I'll never want anything else. She practically danced all the way down Evans Road under the stark bare branches of the giant trees. I'm going to the dance with Michael, she whispered, hugging her secret to her heart.

19

"Alicia, you can hand me the wreath now—the hook's still firm from last year," Denne said reaching down from the ladder where she perched in front of the fireplace.

Alicia handed her the big wreath, stifling a yawn as she did so.

"I really appreciate you girls' getting up on Saturday morning to help me decorate," Margaret said. "I promise you a big brunch of waffles and sausage as soon as we're finished." She busily took the lids off several more boxes of decorations. "I'll be so happy to have the house all decorated for Christmas when the Dodsons come for dinner tonight."

Denne chuckled. "Face it, Mom, that's just an excuse. You always want to decorate for Christmas the minute Thanksgiving is over."

"That's true, I guess," Margaret laughed. "I just

love everything about Christmas and I like to make it last as long as possible." She went to the stereo in the corner. "In fact, why don't we have a little Christmas music to really get us into the mood?"

Alicia groaned. "Can we stand the strains of 'The Little Drummer Boy' so early in the morning?"

"It's good for you to get up early once in a while," Denne said as she climbed down the ladder and tackled the metallic strings of gold garland. "You might get a whole new perspective on life."

"I like the one I get a little later in the day," Alicia grumped, lazily opening the box of little Santa and elves candleholders. "After all, I need to get my beauty sleep if I'm going to compete with Kristin Granville."

"I don't think I've ever heard of her," Margaret said. "Denne, how do you think it'd look to drape some of those above the wreath on the fireplace?"

"I don't have any hooks to hold it, Mom," Denne replied. "But I can put some here, right along the mantel." She held the glittering strands in a looped design.

Alicia stared into the distance at an imaginary Kristin Granville, totally oblivious to the decorating problems. "She just came here from Chicago and she is absolutely the most beautiful girl in school. She's only been here a week and every single student at Clinton High knows who she is."

"Well, I doubt that you have anything to worry about, dear," Margaret smiled. "Everyone has known who you are for a long time." She nodded at Denne. "Right," she said. "That looks perfect."

Margaret turned back to the brooding Alicia.

"Do you have two dates with two different boys today, as usual?" Margaret queried.

"No, just one," Alicia replied, "I'm going to dinner and a movie with Brad."

"What's going on, anyway?" Margaret asked as she began moving knickknacks from the lamp table to the closed cabinet below the bookcase. "Has Brad replaced Michael completely? I never hear anything about Michael anymore?"

"Well, it's his own fault," Alicia said flatly. "He hasn't asked me out for a couple of weeks now, and Brad has. As a matter of fact, he asked me to the Winter Dinner Dance," she said with a satisfied smile. She arranged a Santa and two elves on the table Margaret had just cleared, then stood back to admire the effect.

At the mention of the dance Denne's heart leaped into her throat, but she kept perfectly quiet. She had told no one—not even her mother or Sharon—about Michael's invitation. She just couldn't bear to share that news, it still seemed more dream than reality. It'd be just my luck for something to happen to change all the plans, she thought, and I'd be so embarrassed I couldn't stand it. Firmly she closed her lips and drove the tiny tacks to hold the roping on the mantel's edge.

"I think Brad *has* replaced Michael if he's taking you to the big dance," Margaret exclaimed. "Speaking of the dance; it's almost here. Isn't it next Friday night?"

Alicia nodded.

"What are you going to wear, Alicia? Do you need a new dress?"

Denne held her breath for fear that Margaret would mention the new velveteen dress and get them into a discussion of whether Denne was going to the dance and with whom, but she didn't. She's too tactful, Denne thought. She'll get me alone soon and tell me again to go to the dance with Jeff, but she doesn't want to bring up my dateless situation in front of Alicia.

"I saw a dress in Nancy's Boutique that'll be perfect," Alicia said. "I've been intending to mention it to you, Mom. I've already tried it on."

"I'm sure you have," Margaret replied, smiling. "All right, I'll go with you to see it one afternoon next week." She opened another box of decorations. "Well, we're going to miss Michael around here," she said. "I've always thought he was such a nice boy."

"Oh, you won't miss him, Mom," Alicia assured her. "You'll get to see him when he comes for his tutoring sessions." She added another Santa to the group, then took it away again, frowning at the little figurines on the table. "Besides, we haven't broken up completely, we've just agreed to date other people, too. I'm sure he'll ask me out again soon," she said confidently.

Denne hung the last loop of the golden garland, her heart in her mouth at Alicia's last words. Alicia sounded so positive it made her want to announce that Michael had asked her to the Winter Dinner Dance. The expression on Alicia's face at that news would be priceless. She held the words back though, still hardly able to believe the invitation herself, haunted by the possibility that her dream might not come true after all.

Monday afternoon Denne hurried into the house, running up the stairs before she even took off her coat. Margaret's voice floated up to her from the sun porch.

"Denne? Aren't you early?"

"Yes, Mom, talk to you in a minute," she answered, going straight to her room.

Denne threw her books and coat onto her desk and began taking off her plaid wool slacks and moss-green sweater. She changed to her new jeans and top, then stood before her mirror and looked at the smiling girl reflected there. The smooth cotton of the tight long-sleeved top fit smoothly over her high rounded breasts and slim arms, and the bright red color brought out the color in her cheeks. They were bright pink and her eyes sparkled. That's from my walk in the cold, she thought. Maybe it's also from the fact that Michael will arrive in just a few minutes.

Giving herself a confident wave, she grabbed her French book and went downstairs to talk with her mother until Michael arrived for his lesson.

Margaret looked up with a smile from the flowered fabric piled on the machine. "Are you tutoring today?" she asked, ripping out some stitches efficiently.

"Yes, Michael will be here in a few minutes," Denne answered. "He's having a conference with Mme Clouet right now—that's why I'm home a little early. It's the week for individual conferences."

Just saying Michael's name out loud was a thrill and she felt her cheeks grow even pinker. I wonder if Mom notices anything, she thought. I wonder if she can hear a difference in my voice when I say his name or if she sees me blush. I wonder if I sound as happy as I feel. Suddenly the thought of seeing

Michael in the next few minutes was so exciting that Denne had an urge to turn cartwheels into the kitchen and back. That I'm sure she'd notice, she smiled to herself. If I did that I'd have to tell her my secret for sure.

"Why don't you go get yourself a snack and come talk with me for a few minutes?" her mother asked, starting to sew the seam again. "Alicia will be here in a little while and I'm going with her to look at that dress at Nancy's Boutique, but I want to get as much of this done as I can before we go."

Denne went into the kitchen and took the milk from the refrigerator. While she poured herself a glass she lifted the lid of the cookie jar and the aroma of sugar cookies floated out to her.

"Mmm, my favorites," she called to Margaret.

The slamming of the front door drowned out her words. The next noise was a slam, too, the sound of Alicia's books hitting the hall table. Alicia stormed into the kitchen, her eyes blazing.

"Mom!" she called loudly.

Margaret appeared in the sun porch door, her eyes wide with astonishment and curiosity.

"Alicia, what on earth . . ." she began.

Alicia cut her off. "I have to make a phone call before we go shopping, Mom," she announced, tears trembling on her long lashes. "There's no point in buying a dress for the dance if I don't have a date."

Both Margaret and Denne stared speechlessly at Alicia. The thought of Alicia without a date for something as important as the Winter Dinner Dance was so incomprehensible that for a moment it was as if she had spoken to them in a language they didn't understand.

Margaret recovered first. "Whatever are you talking about?" she demanded.

"I was at my locker after school," Alicia began, leaning against the counter for support, "and I heard Brad's name mentioned, so I started to listen. That new girl, Kristin Granville, was talking to Linda Fowler at her locker which is right next to mine. She was so excited because today someone asked her to the Winter Dinner Dance. And guess who that someone was? Brad Fitzgerald!"

Alicia's beautiful wide eyes, dark blue with emotion, looked from her mother to her sister and back again.

"Can you imagine?" she demanded. "I know Brad thinks Kristin is really pretty—I heard a couple of remarks he made to Don the other day, but I can't believe he'd do this to me. I just can't believe it!" She hit the counter top with her small fist.

"Alicia, calm down," Margaret said. "You may have misunderstood the entire conversation. Now you just stop getting so upset and get this whole matter straightened out before you work yourself into a real fit." She walked over to Alicia and put her arm around her shoulders. "Come on honey," she said calmly, "don't be so upset. I think this is all just a mix-up of some kind."

"Well, mix-up or whatever, I intend to find out!" Alicia declared. "Brad is at work right now, but I'm going to call him anyway." She dashed to the hallway to phone, leaving Denne and Margaret standing in the kitchen dumbfounded.

Absentmindedly, Denne took a cookie and started munching, giving Margaret a quizzical look. "What do you think, Mom? Would Brad really do that?"

"Oh, surely not," she answered, returning to the sun porch and her sewing. "He seems like a really nice boy."

Denne picked up her glass and followed her mother. She was caught up in Alicia's dilemma, her mind whirling with all the possibilities. She sat down and slowly drank her milk while she considered that Alicia might really be without a date for the Winter Dinner Dance. What irony! she thought. I have a date for the dance and Alicia may not. That's certainly a switch!

Soon the murmur of Alicia's voice stopped. There was a silence, then suddenly she was framed in the doorway, the weak winter sunlight glinting off her shining hair. Her eyes were wide with tragedy, tears beginning to roll down her cheeks.

"It's true," she whispered, her hurt look locking with Margaret's incredulous one. "Brad said he was planning to tell me tonight." Blindly she sank into the chair nearest the door.

Denne didn't know what to say; suddenly she felt very sorry for her sister. Alicia looked absolutely crushed huddled in the big cushions of the chair—Denne had never seen her so sad.

Margaret moved to comfort Alicia, going to sit on the ottoman at her feet. Alicia's voice broke as she asked her mother, "How can he do this to me?" Without giving Margaret time to answer, Alicia went on, talking to no one in particular. "I thought he really liked me; I thought we'd be going together all the rest of this year, at least. . . ." She stared into space, brushing at a tear, then twisting the end of the long braid that held her hair away from her face on one side.

"He was going to tell me tonight," she repeated.

She looked from Margaret to Denne and back again, emphasizing each word. "He was going to tell me tonight and the dance is only four days away!" Her voice rose with disbelief, then cracked with anger.

Alicia sat up straight, horrified as the full reality of the situation hit her. "That makes me furious! He is giving me four days to find another date for the most important event of the school year!" She gripped the rattan arms of the chair, her wide eyes on Margaret's.

"Mom," she said desperately, "I have to go. I have to go and I have to have a date."

Margaret tried to comfort her. "Now, Alicia, I'm sure there are still some boys who haven't asked anyone yet. . . ."

Her words didn't register with Alicia; another implication of the disaster had hit her. "Ooh, Demoiselles," she wailed. "Everyone of the members will have a date to the dance, and I won't. And I'm the president of the club!" She bit her lip. "How embarrassing can that be!" Then, belatedly, Alicia realized what Margaret had said.

"That's it!" she cried, jumping up from her chair and beginning to pace around the room. "I have to think of someone who doesn't have a date yet; there must be *someone* I know." Alicia's jaw set determinedly.

She looks much more like herself, Denne thought. She certainly doesn't stay crushed for long.

"I know!" Alicia said happily. "Michael can take me. I just know he would have asked me if Brad hadn't asked me first. I'll bet he doesn't have a date yet."

Denne's heart stopped. She opened her mouth to say that Michael had asked her to the dance; that

Michael already had a date, but she closed it again. Alicia was right. No doubt Michael would have taken her to the dance if Brad hadn't asked first; he had only asked Denne on the rebound. In fact, Denne thought, sick inside at the idea, he may have just asked me to get back at Alicia for dating Brad in the first place. Alicia was prattling on, but Denne couldn't bring herself to stop her. He'll drop me and take her, she thought, going all empty inside. He's always been crazy about Alicia and if he sees a chance to get her back, he'll take it. Alicia's words echoed Denne's thoughts.

"Michael has always cared a lot for me," she was musing. "He's just been upset because I wanted to go with Brad, too. I'll apologize to him and be very sweet. I'll explain that I've thought it over and decided that I don't want us to date other people after all," Alicia said decisively, as if the matter were settled. Then she really looked at Denne for the first time that afternoon. "Isn't Michael coming over later for a tutoring session?" she asked.

Denne stared at her, eyes wide, barely able to think, much less to speak. Finally, very quietly, she said, "Yes."

"Listen, Denne, tell him that I have to talk to him. Tell him it's very important, that . . ."

The sound of the doorbell interrupted her instructions.

"I'm sure that's Michael now," Denne said hoarsely, forcing the words around the lump in her throat.

Alicia's hands flew to her hair, then to her wrinkled skirt. "Oh, I look like an absolute mess," she said worriedly. "I'll tell you what, Denne," now her tone was that of a fellow conspirator, "you go ahead and have the tutoring session and let me have time to wash my face and brush my hair. Tell Michael to wait in the den when you're finished and then come get me, O.K.?"

Numbly, Denne nodded. Alicia rushed for the stairs.

20

Denne opened the front door and the sight of Michael's handsome smile went straight to her heart.

"Hi, Den," he said brightly, handing her his books to hold while he took off his coat. "You're going to be so proud of how well I know this lesson. In fact, I'll bet you'll reward me with hot chocolate and cookies after the work is all done!"

His words and the warm way he said them filled her with such a bittersweet pain that tears came to her eyes. She looked down quickly and tried to blink them away while he bent over to give Muffin's ears a tug. He stood and took back his books, but still she couldn't speak—the lump in her throat had grown every second that he'd been there.

"Hey, what do you say?" he asked. "Do you have some extra time for me today?"

Denne nodded and forced out a strange sound. She cleared her throat and tried again.

"I have the time," she murmured painfully, "but Alicia wants to talk with you when we're done."

Michael's eyebrows shot up in surprise. "Alicia? Well, all right," he shrugged.

He was indeed well prepared and Denne took him through the exercises as fast as she could, barely succeeding for those few minutes in forcing her attention onto the language and away from Michael and her sister.

At last she closed her book. *"C'est fini,"* she told him. It really is finished, she thought. After this things will be so strained between us I doubt we can even study together.

He reached for her hand. "Don't go yet," he said. "That was a short lesson."

Denne looked into his dark eyes, the feeling of his strong hand making her want to stay with him forever and never let Alicia come in. She couldn't bear to be so near him, though, thinking that soon he would belong to her sister again. She couldn't bear, either, for him to treat her now as if she were his girl when all her practical sense told her that soon he would be treating her as the little sister once more.

"Really, Michael, I think I'd better call Alicia. She's in a hurry to talk with you."

"Well, all right, but you wait for me, O.K? I'm sure whatever she wants won't take too long." He touched Denne's hair lightly.

A thrill of excitement shot through her, then a pang of loss that was just as strong as the excitement had been. The strength of those emotions stretched her nerves so tight that she felt she would burst into tears in the next few seconds.

"O.K., I'll wait," she murmured, and escaped into the hallway.

Alicia was halfway down the stairs. "Are you finished with the lesson?" she asked eagerly, flipping her freshly brushed hair back over her shoulder and biting her glossy lips for color.

"Yes, he's waiting for you," Denne muttered, passing her sister on the staircase as she ran for her room.

She closed the door carefully behind her and stood in the middle of the floor to stare at her reflection in the mirror. I certainly don't look like the same girl who left this room an hour ago, she thought, and I don't feel like her either.

From the corner of her eye she could see the deep blue velveteen dress hanging on the closet door. She took it down and held it in front of her, trying to imagine how it would be to wear the dress and have Michael standing beside her. A terrible wrench twisted inside her. I've dreamed of it for a whole year, she thought, a whole year I've wanted my magical evening with Michael, and I never thought there was the remotest chance it could really come true.

But it almost did! It would have been so perfect, she whispered, so perfect it couldn't really happen.

With a yearning ache in her throat and in her heart, Denne put the dress back and walked to the window. The shadows were long in the light from the lowering sun and the stark branches formed a mixed-up pattern on the snow. Those shadows are just as tangled as my feelings, she whispered and I don't think that any of them can ever be straightened out again.

I should have known it would never work, she thought, leaning against the wall, her eyes staring blindly out the window. He did get to know me as a person and he did care about my feelings, but he's always thought Alicia was wonderful. He probably only turned to me because she was hurting him and we were together so much. Now that she wants him back I can't compete with her. I knew the first time I saw him that he was much too handsome and too popular to be interested in someone like me. This whole thing has been just a wild and silly dream that I should have blotted out of my mind the minute it first appeared.

Resolutely, she straightened. I have to overcome it, she told herself. I'm going to make a life of my own; I'm going to develop my own individual self. After all, I have my scholarship challenge to look forward to—getting ready for those exams will keep me so busy I won't have time to think about Michael or Alicia. And if I win it, I can look forward to a whole wonderful year in France!

Even that exciting thought couldn't keep her mind away from the present, however, and she wandered back to the blue dress, lightly touching its folds hanging softly against the white of the door. It's a shame to waste it, she murmured. Maybe I should follow Mom's advice and ask Jeff whether he already has a date. I know he was going to ask me that day when Michael walked up to my locker.

She visualized Jeff's clear gray eyes on hers and his nervousness as he'd tried to talk with her that day and she knew for certain that his feelings for her ran deep. He really likes me, she thought, as she slumped onto the cheerful quilt that covered her bed.

Denne stretched out on her back and stared intensely at the ceiling. I can't do that to him, she said at last, trying not to look toward the blue dress. Eventually I would put him through the same kind of hurt I'm going through now, and I just can't do it to him. Jeff is too good a person and too good a friend, and even if he weren't, nobody deserves to hurt like this.

Deliberately she forced herself to look at the velveteen dress. I was going to wear that dress for my dream evening with Michael and if I can't be with him I'll stay home, she whispered. The sound of his name on her lips made her relive once more the glorious feeling of his lean body so close to hers as he grinned down at her and asked her to the dance. The tones of his voice came back to her and the look in his dark eyes was real all over again. She thought of the sweet warmth and the burning excitement in his kiss, the delicious feeling of his lips on hers and she melted as if he were there with her again.

Hurt stabbed her and she threw herself off the bed and onto her feet, pacing restlessly to the window again. Tears stung her eyelids but she brushed them away and swallowed hard, determined not to have a tear-stained face when she talked to him. Oh why, *why* did I say I'd wait for him? she asked herself in frustration. I don't think I can talk to him without crying—it'll all be just that much worse.

She pressed her forehead against the cold glass of the window, one knee resting on the window seat. Dusk was falling, but she could still see the branches and their faint shadows, shades of gray on the white of the snow-covered ground. In all the white and gray she could see one small dot of color. It was a cardinal, hopping from one branch to another and then to the ground, pecking as if it were looking for food. The bird was the only moving thing Denne could see in the gathering twilight and its loneliness pulled at a kindred feeling in her.

"I'll feed you," she called softly. "Wait just a minute; I'm coming."

Not stopping to exchange her loafers for boots, Denne shrugged into her furry rabbit-skin jacket and went down the stairs toward the sack of birdseed in the kitchen. The door to the den was still closed and she hurried past it, hoping she could get outside before it opened. I won't wait for him, she thought suddenly. I just can't see him again today; in fact, I don't think I can talk to him ever again.

She went into a bright, good-smelling kitchen that seemed like an alien world.

"Well, hi, honey," Margaret said, "I was wondering where you were." Her eyebrows lifted in surprise at the sight of Denne's coat. "Are you going somewhere?"

"Just to put out a little birdseed," Denne muttered, sticking her head into the cabinet to avoid her mother's glance. "I saw a red bird from my window who looks hungry." She poured some of the feed into a bowl and left hurriedly.

The cold air was a shock and Denne pulled up her fur hood. More than the cold, though, it was the feeling of late afternoon in winter that made her shiver. This is the sad time of day, she thought, the in-between day and night time that makes everything seem gloomy.

The cardinal was sitting on the perch of the empty

bird feeder, pecking disconsolately at a few empty sunflower-seed shells. He flew up to one of the tree limbs as Denne approached and she removed the lid and filled the feeder, watching the mixed seeds flow into it. She made the job last as long as she could, but soon it was full and she replaced the top. She looked up into the bare branches and called, "All right, now, you can come back and have some dinner." The bird was barely visible in the darkening shadows.

Slowly Denne walked to the trunk of the big tree and leaned against it while she waited to see whether the bird would eat. As always the tree radiated comfort to her and she pressed her back against its secure bulk.

After a moment or two, the chill beginning to numb her feet and the darkening gloom made the lights of the house very inviting, but she dreaded going back in. Maybe he'll go soon, she thought, maybe I can stay out here until he leaves and I won't have to see him again.

She rubbed her fingers over the rough bark of the huge old tree, then thrust her hands into her pockets to warm them. I'll have to go in pretty soon, though, she thought. I'm just not dressed for this.

At last the bird hopped onto the perch of the feeder again, and she watched it begin to eat, its color almost lost now as the light failed. She tried to force her thoughts to stay with the bird and away from Michael, but she no longer could.

Once more the memory of his kiss floated into her mind. She leaned her head back against the tree trunk and, closing her eyes, floated out of the present back into that magic time. The feel of his lips on hers a sweet thrill once more.

Suddenly she heard the crunch of footsteps. She didn't open her eyes, she just waited for Margaret's voice to ask her why she was standing out here in the snow all alone. The footsteps stopped but her mother's voice never came.

She opened her eyes. Michael was standing very near, his mouth curved in a smile so warm that it removed all the cold from her body.

"When I asked you to wait I had no idea you would be out here," he teased. "Aren't you about to freeze?"

She couldn't answer. She simply looked at him, her heart pounding so loudly she was sure he must be able to hear it.

He moved to her, putting his hands on the trunk of the tree on each side of her. He moved his face close to hers, watching every detail of her expression in the dusky light.

"Denne . . ." he said, and her heart stopped. She waited for him to ask her to release him from their date. She looked down, shading her eyes with her long lashes, trying not to cry.

He put his hand under her chin and tilted her head up.

"I need to know what color you're going to wear on Friday," he said. "I'm going to order your flowers tomorrow."

Her heart began beating again, this time with a joy that pulsed through her entire body like a song.

"Oh, Michael," she whispered, as she threw her arms around his neck and hugged him with all her might

First Love from Silhouette

This Month's Titles

It's My Turn by Eleni Carr

A move from a small town to a big city can certainly change a person's life, especially when you're sixteen and don't like the idea. Soon she found that there was more to it than just changing schools and adapting to a new environment. There were exciting, new friendships—such as with worldly, disillusioned Seth, and her friendly classmate, Rick. Would either be the boy of her choice?

In My Sister's Shadow by Genell Dellin

Dennie couldn't stand always being compared to her older sister! She decided to earn recognition for herself in the only area she could do better—her studies. But she was distracted by a tall, blond boy with dark eyes, her sister's boyfriend, Michael. A chance to tutor him had led to an unexpected friendship. How could she ever compete with her glamorous sister for the most wonderful boy in the world?